LEAP YEAR BLOOD LUST

Vera M Murray

Copyright © Vera (Veronica) M Murray, 2011, 2019

All rights reserved. No part of this publication may be reproduced, stored in a retrieval system, or transmitted in any form or by any means without the prior written permission of the copyright owner, through the publisher, nor be otherwise circulated in any form of binding or cover other than that in which it is published and without a similar condition being imposed on the subsequent purchaser.

Assisted by Bent Banana Books, 24 Lorraine Court, Lawnton, Qld, Australia 4501.

All characters, events, and places recorded in this publication are fictitious and any resemblance to real persons, living or dead, is purely coincidental.

A CiP Catalogue record for this book is available from the Australian National Library.

IBSN No: 978-0-9872784-0-1 (paperback)

Author: Vera M Murray, 4 Leis Parade, Lawnton. Queensland, 4501, Australia 2011

Cover design: Ken Armstrong.
Additional cover design: Ian Curr
Back cover photo: Bernie Dowling

Dedicated to my children:

Joanne Croyden, Frank Fisk, and their families

FOLLOWING ON FROM THE TRAGEDY THAT STRUCK ROCKVILLE

IN THE LEAP YEAR OF 1988

A mutilated body was found in

ROCKVILLE

On each following leap year

FROM 1992

The victims were –

John Allen 1992

James Allen 1996

Patrick Allen 2000

Note: Taken from the Greystone police records

IN THE LEAP YEAR OF 2004

THE EVIL ONES

LAUGH AND WAIT;

INTENT ON

DEALING OUT DEATH

TO THE NEXT

WITH THE MARK OF THE VICTIM

BOOK 1

'There are more things in heaven and earth Horatio, than are dreamt of in your philosophy.'

From: Shakespeare's *Hamlet.*

CHAPTER 1

Thomas Allen answers the call.

Tom Allen had a strong feeling he was being followed and closely watched. As he drove, he kept glancing through the rear vision mirror and the side windows of his Holden sedan in turn. With all senses alert, he sped along the Rockville section of the road between the small coastal towns of Little Rock and Greystone. Although a two-lane road it was narrow and devoid of buildings of any description on either side. It was unsealed, as it merely linked a chain of small west coast towns strung along the edge of the coastal fringe facing the sea.

To ease his anxiety, and dismiss what he now considered merely a lapse in concentration, he quickly reached into the glove box to locate a fresh packet of cigarettes. In this clumsy attempt, several army badges fell out. Glancing at them as they dropped to the floor, his unnatural nervousness ignited sparks in his memory. They kindled into a flame, causing the past to burn bright in his mind's eye. He pictured the punch-up, the fast movement of his fist as he lashed out, then his unconscious Colonel's bloody face. His superior officer had had the nerve to try to stop a drunken brawl in the barracks. The result, after that event had been added to a list of other reckless episodes, attracted a dishonourable discharge.

'One day your drinking problem will lead you into the kind of trouble you won't be able to get out of, Thomas Allen. Mark my words.' That was his Major's farewell message.

Tom was aware that his drink-fuelled temper could get the best of him. His three marriage break-ups, plus the shameful ending of his army career, were proof of this. His army doctor's prediction that Tom would die within two years if he continued drinking alcohol, was evidence of his excesses. He grimaced as he realised those two years were up, on this very day, February 29, 2004, a leap year.

The ex-soldier told himself to relax. He asked himself, 'Who'd have thought I'd end up doing the kind of job I'm doing now?' Free, and having no close relatives to consider, he had accepted the position of travelling sales Representative for the Home Appliances and House Improvement Company. His territory consisted of a string of coastal towns and an adjoining strip of rural land. This type of job suited his forceful nature – what others called, 'his pushy manner and polished standover tactics'. It could also be regarded as highly developed sales skills. Tom grimaced. *My co-workers have always been envious of my success.*

He shrugged and flicked back the strands of blond hair that kept falling forward and into his eyes. 'I suppose I shouldn't drink so much,' he thought, but he knew it was too late for regret – not that he had ever seriously entertained such an idea. Most of his present job contacts were acquired while frequenting hotel bars.

As if to reassure himself, he patted the briefcase beside him. Inside were several contracts, lying snugly, waiting for completion. 'A very successful day,' he announced to the empty air. He had proved once again he was a great asset to the firm.

His stomach rumbled, directing his thoughts to food and whiskey. He wondered if Madeline, the barmaid at Greystone's Boulder Hotel where he was based, was on duty. His eyes glazed over as he pictured her tiny face framed by wisps of blond hair, then to her inviting lips. He further visualised her trim body – her shapely legs. He told himself that, at last he had found his one and only lasting true love, ignoring the fact that he had thought the same on several other occasions.

His mind recalled his doctor forecasting a reasonable short life for him. It had made him think that his belongings and savings would end up in government coffers, so he made a will leaving everything he owned to Madeline. *I won't be telling her. That's my secret. From my experience with women, they're quick to disappear out of your life if something comes up that doesn't suit them, especially if you're caught with someone else. I think Madeline's different, but if she doesn't know about it, it won't have any impact should we break up. I'd just cancel it . . . make a new one.*

Reluctantly, he dismissed those thoughts. Business was more important. Tom glanced at his gold Rolex watch. He told himself he still had time to make one more call before turning in for the day. He decided to visit the farmhouse he had glimpsed further back and off the road – if he could locate the entrance to the side road. There were many trees along its frontage. *The dirt track into it may be marked on my map.*

He directed the car to the side of the road and turned off the engine. Picking up his dog-eared area map, he flicked it open. Turning to the local district page his eyes fixed on an unfamiliar turn-off ahead, winding off to a seaside town called Rockville. It was a name he had never noticed on the map before, nor ever heard mentioned. He considered his two choices. He toyed with the options of whether to turn back and search for the farmhouse, or make a visit to Rockville.

I'll catch up on the farmhouse tomorrow. A small town's a cert for business. I'll call in, make the acquaintance of the publican, hint for business and see what comes up.

He was well aware that in such tiny towns many of the menfolk dribbled through the hotel at some time, either during the day or after work. If their usual social gathering at the local 'watering hole' was later rather than earlier, he could stay the night. His expense account covered such occasions.

He restarted his car and cruised, keeping a keen eye out for the in-road. He spotted a signpost some distance ahead, which read 'ROCKVILLE,' in large print, and an arrow pointing down a side road. He wondered why he had not noticed it before. *Perhaps it's new.*

Before he indicated, he noticed that dusk had begun to spread its grey sun-sinking wings over the land. Tom shivered and the desire for a drink and a tender steak, followed by the pleasure of the compliant Madeline, caused him to re-think. *I'll bypass Rockville – leave it for today. I'll check the sign and the entrance road for next time.*

He cruised on. A short distance past the sign, the lights of a speeding vehicle coming from the opposite direction momentarily blinded him. *What idiot puts his high beam on when it's hardly dark? Perhaps his windscreen wipers aren't working and the bit of rain that's coming down's affecting his vision.*

The vehicle seemed to be aiming straight for him. Tom instinctively swerved. *Hell!* His mind silently screamed in disbelief as his sweaty hands slipped, releasing their grip of the steering wheel. His car's erratic behaviour caused it to veer across both lanes. He had now passed the Rockville turnoff.

He gave vent to his anger by shouting profanities at the car driver, now out of sight. He tried to regain control of the car while the roar of several motors pounded his ears as they passed. They were competing it seemed, for supremacy above his own shrieks. As the sounds echoed around inside the car they seemed to include high-pitched, uncanny, blood-chilling laughter. *Now I'm hearing things. I'm going bonkers.*

Controlling the rising panic, he felt his fingers further tighten their grip on the wheel in his fight against what could become his metal casket. The instinct to survive gained strength. It allowed him to retake control as the car jumped on to the rough verge of the road. It bounced along lumpy ground, shaking the very innards of both car and driver.

His foot pinned the brake hard to the floor. The car came to a tyre-burning stop, its front wheels spinning aimlessly in a shallow depression. Tom's body was jolted forward by the abrupt halt. His forehead hit the steering wheel. The pain caused the world to become blurred. He slumped down in the seat, breathing heavily and again mouthing expletives. The noise made by passing cars faded, but the mad laughter returned. Tom covered his ears to smother the sound. When he could no longer hear anything, he allowed his arms to drop to his sides.

In the ensuring silence a further pain rose to engulf him. He felt as if a knife had pierced his right eye. He assumed his sunglasses had broken when his face hit the steering wheel. Tom could not hear the words that immediately exploded from within, until they became a scream. "AAHH . . . AAHH . . . !" His hands shielded his face in a futile attempt to protect it from the damage already done.

His mind was still in turmoil as he felt another knife cut across his lower stomach. *What demon's torturing me?* He jerked his head back against the seat's leather headrest, as the pain in his head remained his main worry. His face twisted and turned from side to side as the flashes of pain intensified along his tender nerve endings. In fierce desperation he clawed fiercely at his face with his nails in an effort to drag away the pain. Blood trickled down his cheeks, to develop into large red angry drops, and soaked into the front of his white silk shirt. As his body doubled up with pain, his head contacted the steering wheel. It caused blood to drip onto, and stain, its fabric cover.

He swung his head painfully around, but his view was too limited – his vision too blurred. "I know someone's responsible for all this. Whoever you are, whoever's doing this, get from wherever you're hiding before I find you and drag you out." There was silence. He twisted his body to glance behind him through eyes, which now had reduced visibility. He seemed to be alone. "Okay, it's off to the police station." Leaning forward he tried to restart the car but the engine refused to turn over. *I'll have to hail a passing car if I want help. I must get this maniac arrested.*

He was still not thinking clearly as he painfully flung open his door, intent on searching the floor of the back seat, believing his vision may have been too blurred earlier to see if anyone was hiding there. Tom carefully swung his legs out, but when he attempted to stand they gave way. Dazed, he crumpled to the ground. Crab-like he crawled to the edge of the road itself, where he rolled on his back to ease his hands and body from contact with the rough ground.

Slowly he forced both eyelids to lift further, for he suspected he could be experiencing a final glimpse of the world he knew. He shouted. "Okay, whoever's there . . . whoever you are . . . show yourself." There was no answer, and no sound came from inside the car. He strained to peer through the light rain now falling, to view the world around him more clearly. A hissing sound made him dispassionately turn his gaze to watch his car's front tyre slowly deflating. Regret that he had left anything to do with vehicles to others in the army, passed swiftly over him. That occupation had belonged to another unit, and he had had no need, nor felt it necessary, to trouble himself with what he considered to be strictly a motor mechanic's job. There had always been someone else to take care of such things.

He lay still, breathing deeply. He suddenly felt isolated from the rest of humanity – the only one left alive in some twilight phantom existence. When the throbbing pains subsided, he gingerly got to his feet. He swayed for a few moments as the unexplained weakness in his legs threatened to overbalance him once again. With one bloody hand clutching his face and the other pressed against his stomach, he began to drag himself one step at a time, away from his car, to be clearly visible to any passing motorist.

Tom waved groggily at the odd speeding vehicle in the half-held belief one would contain a Good Samaritan and stop. He remembered hearing it mentioned that this quiet, deserted stretch of road between Little Rock and Greystone had a bad reputation. 'Spooky,' said some drivers who told stories of past mysterious deaths on this section of coast. Some drivers could not get through it quickly enough.

Tom began to beckon the next passing car, but the driver accelerated when he had him in his sights. Turning towards the dying sun, he screamed out every swear word he knew for the whole world to feel his anger, especially drivers with no compassion.

Trapped in his own despair, his mind battled to retain his now wavering grip on reality. He abandoned his futile efforts to attract the attention of any passing driver. *How else can I get help? A* feeling of urgency had risen. He feared he might be there all night. He began to seek inspiration. Looking back the way he had come, his eyes picked up the Rockville sign he had noticed earlier. Tom stumbled back towards it. *Whoever has caused this can stay marooned. I'll walk to Rockville and hope it's reasonably close. They'll have a medical centre there for sure.* To find a doctor was his first priority, convinced now he was suffering some kind of seizure from the head trauma.

Halting regularly, he covered the distance back to the signpost. There he sucked in fresh cool air to give himself the strength and confidence to keep his eyes open. Squinting now, but still with blurred vision, he fought to focus on the sign itself. The words gradually became clearer.

ROCKVILLE – 1.5km.

Although now more mentally alert, Tom's physical weakness was still paramount. His legs again betrayed him. He attempted to grip the signpost to prevent himself from slamming into the soaked ground, but it was too late. His hand slipped, and he fell. His head contacted the sharp edge of the post. Blackness threatened to engulf him as he slid to the ground. He stiffened in protest at the severe pain spearing through his bashed forehead and stomach area.

With his body soaked in sweat and light rain, he became aware that the tormenting pain was ebbing. He began tentatively to check his face and head. His probing fingers found a fresh cut beginning to ooze blood.

He struggled to his feet. He pressed his weight on each leg separately to gauge their strength. They were steady enough he decided. Although his vision was still blurred he was confident that he could walk the distance to Rockville. The sharpest pains in his body had diminished considerably and could almost be tolerated.

I need a doctor. Rockville seems to be my only hope. He looked back at his stationary vehicle. *But the sooner I get help the better, before it gets too dark. There's no public phone on this road to call for help like on the main highways. My phone! It's still in the car.* 'Damn it!' The words spat from his mouth. "I must be off with the fairies not to think of it before."

He attempted to return to his car, turning his back on the sign and the turnoff to Rockville, but he found he could not step forward. Some invisible barrier prevented him from moving in that direction. It put him in mind of the treadmill in the gym – running on the spot and getting nowhere. He thrust his body forward but was unsuccessful. It proved to be impossible. Creeping panic began to take over. *It's as if an invisible 'force field's stopping me. Now I'm thinking Star Trek. My mind's going. I need a doctor as quick as I can. If I've had some sort of turn, I don't want a repetition. Then I'll get a mechanic to bring me back and change the tyre so I can get moving again.*

Tom turned to face down the Rockville road. A hesitant step forward proved he was able to proceed down that road, but prevented from making any headway in the direction of the Holden.

That cursed signpost seems to want to keep me here. Weird, it's like I'm metal and being drawn by a magnet . . . to Rockville . . . as if I have no choice. Rubbish! I'm not thinking straight, but perhaps it's for the best. Rockville isn't that far down the track.

Tom tried to come to terms with the predicament in which he found himself. He was in a situation out of his control. There was no superior officer on hand to give explanations or bark orders that would be blindly followed. This day's happenings were far from 'laid out'. No recall of standard army procedure covered the present crisis.

A spark of optimism began to repel the depression that had crept over him. He commenced walking between the trees lining each side of Rockville Road. The dirt road was stony; with tufts of grass sprouting in clumps here and there. Tom's thin-soled, handcrafted shoes were threatening to slip and topple him, as the ground had become slippery from the recent shower. More stones appeared, and extended like a carpet, to dissolve into the dark shadows of rugged outcrops. No other landmarks were close enough to discern, except for a low flat-topped mountain directly ahead.

His slow steps made no sound, nor had he heard or seen any birds or wild life. Not even the sound of a barking dog reached him. It was then that he began to notice the oppressive stillness. It seemed unnatural. He did not like it, and began to sense a strangeness about the place. This was reinforced by the fact that no vehicle had passed him, nor were any tracks of any kind to be seen on the ground itself. The landscape in every direction also looked empty. As he drew closer to the base of the levelled mountaintop directly ahead he could just make out in the fading light, ruins proudly perched on top, like a storm-battered, bedraggled sea bird.

Looking around, he found himself staring at a sign reading:

ROCKVILLE, NEXT RIGHT

ROCKVILLE QUARRY NEXT LEFT

He increased his pace, but the effort was short-lived. His body felt unnaturally tired and breathlessness was becoming his greatest burden. He seated himself on a boulder to have another of his countless stops.

His body rested, but his mind kept active. *How did I find myself in this predicament? I'm sitting on a boulder in the middle of nowhere, with a body I feel no longer belongs to me. The smell of the blood on my head and clothes is making me nauseous.*

On checking his watch Tom discovered an hour had passed since leaving his car. The date read February 29, 2004. *There's only one 29th of February in every four years. If this weren't a leap year, I wouldn't be here now.* He smirked at his attempt at light-hearted jest.

Tom became aware that the approaching shadows were about to claim the whole area. As the last of the daylight withdrew, the sun was silhouetting the massive ruins on the peak, against a fading, lemon-tinted sky. He wondered why he had never heard any mention of a derelict house in these parts, but he did not dwell on it.

In the lingering glow Tom could not see any sign of habitation. He had a sinking feeling he was heading towards a ghost town. But, he knew he had to keep moving, before the mist now forming around his legs rose higher.

A large 'Welcome to Rockville' sign in mint condition suddenly confronted him. *That wasn't there before, or was it? Maybe I couldn't see because my eyes are blurry. So the town does exist.* He half-circled the signpost and noticed buildings beginning to appear out of the fog, which as yet, had merely hugged the hollows. *Rockville at last!* Tom hurried on.

Before him, streetlights began to click into life, and comforting orange globes shone here and there through house windows. But, to Tom, the flickering red sign 'Rockville Hotel' had a most welcoming aura about it.

But first the doc! No building looked like a medical centre. No shopfront appeared to have the shine of a doctor's shingle.

As there was no one to be seen in the main street to ask for directions to their medical centre, Tom turned, and steered his unsteady footsteps towards the hotel entrance.

CHAPTER 2

Tomas Allen meets some very unhappy locals

Tom walked up to face the building at close range. *It looks as if it's been up a long time.* The lower floor had been built with stone extracted from the nearby quarries. A long veranda stretched from end to end on the upper floor. It overshadowed the lower level of the building. The railings enclosing it were built of local timber and each paling was vertical, straight, and painted white. Tom breathed deeply with relief when he pushed open the solid pine doors and entered. He stumbled over to the reception desk, where, with his tortured walk behind him, Tom stood as if in a trance. Exhaustion had now wrapped itself tightly around and through him.

    The night clerk, dressed in baggy pants, long sleeved shirt and a waistcoat, hurried towards him. Casting his eyes over the new arrival he gave a low gasp. He stared at the filthy condition Tom was in. Wearing an expression of deep concern he quickly pushed his pen into his waistcoat pocket. "What happened? Are you all right?" he blurted out.

    Tom remained stationary, unwilling to move. He heard the clerk but did not answer. All he was conscious of, was relief to be back in a warm, familiar environment.

    "Take it easy mate. From the look of you, you need to see Doc Jenkins. He's just down the road a bit. I'll take you. By the way, my name's Bill."

    He cupped Tom's elbow with the palm of his hand and gently nudged him back out into the street. He guided Tom to a neat iron-roofed house where a doctor's brass sign reflected their faces as they drew closer. Side by side they climbed the three steps. At the top Bill pushed open the door to the surgery/residence. Inside, Bill rang a small brass bell on the counter, while Tom slumped into an easy chair in the empty waiting room.

Within seconds the doctor made his appearance.

"What's this you've got here Bill?" He asked while surveying the stiff figure sitting awkwardly\y in the chair.

"Hi doc, this guy here just walked into the hotel. He's in bad shape."

"Let's see now." Dr Jenkins walked over to Tom. He waved his hand in front of Tom's eyes. Tom stared vacantly back at him. To Tom, the doctor's voice seemed to be speaking very slowly. "He's sure in a bad state. Could be a case of concussion from that head wound. He's been in some kind of accident obviously." His voice was full of concern.

Well, I sure never did this to myself. "My eyes, doctor, look at my eyes. I'm afraid I'll lose my sight completely," Tom suddenly blurted out. "They've been bleeding . . . look at my shirt. That's blood there. It's also from my head."

The doctor glanced briefly at Tom's clothes. "Yes, there's dried blood, dirt, and grass stains, but first I'm going to ask you a couple of questions to test your awareness. This is just normal procedure. First, do you know where you are?"

"I'm in a doctor's surgery in a place called Rockville."

"Were you in an road accident?"

"Well . . . no . . . yes . . . but . . ." *How can I explain what happened? I don't really know myself.*

The doctor looked at Bill who still hovered in the background. "He'll be fine. I'll send him back when we're finished."

"Right-oh doc."

Bill was about to leave when he turned and called out to the doctor. "Don't forget the send-off for Reverend Anderson. It's probably started by now." A grunt of acknowledgement came from the doctor. The door clicked shut behind Bill.

The doctor returned his attention to Tom. "Would you come this way, please?"

Tom rose stiffly, and followed the doctor into his surgery where he indicated a high padded table.

"Climb up there and I'll check you over. You may have some injuries other than that cut on your head."

Tom slowly climbed up. At the doctor's hand gesture he lay flat on the padded surface. The doctor took his pulse, his blood pressure, and noted his heavy breathing. He then examined his stomach, back and limbs.

He seemed pleased with his findings. "No broken bones, although there are some bruises on your back and knees." He produced a hypodermic needle. "You're suffering from shock, but this will counteract the reaction your body is experiencing." The doctor quickly administered the remedy.

Tom was satisfied that some of his unuttered questions appeared to have been explained away, but the most important ones were yet to be resolved. "What about my face . . . my eyes . . . my stomach?" Tom felt obliged to shout, as the doctor seemed partially deaf. Tom had already dismissed the other jabs his body had been subjected to. His main concern at that moment was for his sight.

The doctor, in response, stared into Tom's eyes. He pressed gently on different parts of his cheeks, while asking if it hurt on those places.

"Not really... only slightly," was always the answer, at which Tom himself was surprised.

He re-examined Tom's scalp. "The cuts are not deep. They'll heal quickly. That duck egg-sized lump will disappear without any adverse effects. There's a few scratches and bruises on your stomach, probably connected to your fall."

"But my eyes?" Tom was becoming impatient at the doctor's seeming lack of concern about what Tom considered the most worrying part of his physical ordeal.

"Are your eyes still worrying you?" asked the doctor as he looked closely into them.

Is this quack blind?

"Look right... no pain?... good... look left... no pain?... good. They're bloodshot but there's no obvious damage apart from a few cuts which are not close enough to either pupil to cause any real damage."

Before Tom could make a stinging reply, the doctor sorted through his stock of medicines until he found a phial of fluid with dropper attached. He returned and squeezed some into Tom's eyes. While Tom blinked away the watery mixture, the doctor smeared cotton wool soaked in some colourless clear fluid over Tom's injuries. "This'll fix the cuts you've sustained and those scratches on your face. They'll heal without leaving any obvious scars."

"Scratches? But the blood stains on my hands... too much blood for scratches, don't you think?" Tom responded, as he brought his hands up closer to the doctor's face.

The doctor took Tom's hands in his, gently turning them over. He caught his breath when he noticed a smudged port-wine star-shaped birthmark on Tom's lower arm. He frowned, lowering Tom's hands as he studied his patient's countenance. He stared at the cornflower blue eyes, the blond unruly hair, and noted the shape of Tom's face, as if he was seeing something that had a profound effect on him.

He was silent for a few moments before he professionally commented, "There're streaks of dried blood on your face and scalp, and some blood residue under your nails. There are bloodstains on your hands and clothes. Something made you scratch your face badly. Perhaps an insect, spider perhaps, crawled on you, although I can't find any rash or bites." He walked to his desk, seated himself and beckoned Tom to join him.

Tom slid from the table. He dressed; then lowered himself into the single available chair. His eyes no longer disturbed him unduly, and he had forgotten the pain he had experienced in his lower abdomen.

"Well, let's get some personal details for the records. What is your name, and occupation?"

"Tom Allen, salesman and ex-army."

"Allen, did you say?" For a moment the doctor faltered, then sucked in his breath. "Have you been to Rockville before?"

"No, I didn't know it existed. Never noticed it on my map of the district before today."

"So, tell me. What made you decide to come here?"

For the next fifteen minutes the doctor heard details of Tom's job, why he was in the area, and what he had experienced on the main road. This included his inability to return to his car, causing him to make the decision to walk to Rockville. He also explained how he felt someone was in the car with him. He claimed he would have seen whoever it was but for his affected vision. His voice trailed off. He told himself he was lucky to be alive.

The doctor listened attentively before observing, "I'm surprised you made it this far after your ordeal, especially with that gale blowing outside. It's enough to blow you off your feet. No wonder you couldn't get back to your car."

"After some light rain earlier it was still as a tomb when I came down the road," insisted Tom.

"It's blowing a gale, like it always does at this time of the year. The fierce winds are, as you are probably aware, well known across this area, it being so close to the sea front. They're more intense in a leap year."

"No," Tom argued. "There wasn't any wind, and I can't hear any now."

The doctor walked to the window. He opened it slightly. The wind whistled as it entered the narrow opening, causing sheets of papers on the doctor's desk to scatter. "Hear the wind now Mr Allen?"

Tom nodded. He had become aware of a thundering roar of surf and wind, as if, united, they were trying to rip the town apart. *Is my mind playing tricks on me again? Is the doctor correct in his prognosis of concussion? I seem to be in a worse state than I thought.* The doctor pulled the window shut.

"Have I been hallucinating about everything? If I wasn't, how do you explain why I didn't feel any wind on the walk down, or when I arrived at the hotel?"

"It's beyond my expertise to give you a professional answer, but personally I would put it down to severe mental and physical shock. That's not uncommon under the circumstances in which you found yourself."

Tom forced himself to control his tongue – realising the futility of pressing the point. *I know what I went through. This man's way off the mark.*

The doctor continued. "Before you, others have experienced the force of the Rockville winds keeping them from going in the direction they wished to go. Considering the state you were in when you arrived, you were without doubt in shock. It would be no surprise to me if you did imagine an attack on your body by some unknown person."

Tom's blood pressure rose. "Are you trying to suggest that I made the whole thing up?"

"Mr. Allen, I'm trying to find a logical answer for your present physical and mental condition," the doctor calmly responded. He rose. "Perhaps I can explain it to you better. Come over here with me to the mirror."

Tom left his chair to join him. Tom could hardly believe what he saw reflected in the mirror. The doctor gently directed his fingers to run down Tom's cheekbones tracing along several red, raised, uneven lines.

"Mr. Allen, look closely. There are four scratches on each side of your face. The marks begin on the forehead, down over the eyelids, touching the bottom of both eyes, and then ending near your chin. They are from your nails obviously. They're superficial injuries Mr. Allen, not deep cuts."

Tom's nerves began to settle down. The doctor was correct. He could see only a small amount of congealed blood on his face, and his shirt was clear except for light smudges.

"There are no actual wounds, other than on your scalp. Nothing substantiates what you believe happened. This doesn't mean I doubt you suffered greatly . . . a psychosomatic condition is what it's called. I have treated ex-military personnel who suffered from that condition."

None of this made sense to Tom, so he changed the subject." I'll have to stay the night it seems. What's the place like here . . . any action?' He winked half-heartedly, knowing that in the state he was in, any 'action' would be out of the question.

The doctor smiled a mirthless smile. "In Rockville we are certain of three things, life in death, death in life, and the daddy of all winds returning every four years. They arrive each leap year, and always at this time of the year. They're always stronger on February 29th. The rest of the time life here is, I like to believe, as uneventful as many other small towns."

He glanced at his wall clock. "I have to leave, but before I go, I wish to make one final comment." This would linger prominently in Tom's mind after he left. The doctor moved closer and spoke almost confidentially. "There are two serious points to consider. If your story is true, there could be something drawing you to Rockville. What you say you experienced could be a premonition of nasty things to come. It may have been a very bad mistake to come into Rockville." He became thoughtful. "Perhaps not. If you're still here in the morning I'm sure you'll have no difficulty getting back to your car and continuing on your way."

Tom tried to dismiss the doctor's rambling, but he still felt a sour emptiness in the base of his stomach. *What does he mean by a premonition? He sure is a weirdo. Nutty as a fruitcake. All I want to do now is get the hell out of Rockville. There's something not right about this place. The hotel clerk and the doctor are still dressing like my father did. It's also too quiet. I'll leave now, not tomorrow. If the doctor has a screw loose, who knows what the rest of them might be like?* But he knew he would not be able to find his way back to his car in the dark. *In this god-forsaken place there doesn't seem to be any streetlights other than those in the town centre.*

"Doctor, may I use your 'phone?"

"Sorry son, wish I could help, but the 'phones are out. We're cut off from the outside world. It happens at this time in every leap year."

If they know this happens every four years, why can't they be prepared and have everything fixed during the other three years between?

"You must have a mobile surely."

"Mobile? No one here has one."

Strewth, what kind of a place is this? "What about a motor mechanic? I need one to get my car back on the road. I'll pay well for the inconvenience."

"Sorry." He sounded sincere. "I believe there's only the odd vehicle here now so we have no mechanics. One would come from Greystone, our nearest town, if we should need one. We have in the past often used the quarry mini-bus, but unfortunately, it's out of use. The sea air rusts metal very quickly"

Tom remained silent, as he could not think of anything more to say. His desire for a measure of strong whiskey now overrode any other considerations.

The doctor picked up a bottle containing tablets. "Take two of these now and two more at two-hour intervals after you get back to the hotel."

After swallowing the two the doctor gave him, Tom pocketed the remainder. There was nothing more Tom wanted than to follow up those pills with an alcoholic chaser.

The hotel seems clean enough. Early tomorrow I'll walk back to my car and use my mobile, if my car hasn't been stripped overnight. I still can't think why I didn't use my phone. Something seemed to have put a block on my memory.

"What do I owe you doc?"

"Nothing. The Lord of the Manor, Lord Flurice Westley, employs me. He owns everything here. He pays me,"

Lord Westley . . . a Lord here . . . interesting. I'll have to make some enquiries. Best to wait 'till I'm in the pub. When Tom stepped out into the night, leaving the clinic behind him, the fierce wind blasted him. He recalled his earlier entrance to the town. If there had been a strong wind then, he would have known. He did not believe he had been so stunned by his experience, that he would forget a wind with such force. 'Odd', he muttered as he leaned forward against its teasing thrust. 'Very odd . . . unreal.'

He was relieved when he reached the broad wooden steps of the hotel. It offered instant shelter, covered as it was by a canvas awning. He hurried inside and strolled across the red plush carpet to Bill who was seated behind the reception desk.

At the sound of footsteps Bill raised his head to survey the returned visitor. "You look a lot better now,

Mr Allen. May I ask if you've been to Rockville before? You remind me of someone with those . . . what Aunt Mavis calls . . . cornflower blue eyes. I've seen the same fair unruly blond hair on someone before too."

Tom automatically brushed back a wayward lock of his hair, but remained silent. *Oh great . . . another one . . . blond hair must be rare in these parts, but who cares?* He took his room keys from Bill and began moving away.

"Perhaps you have a close relative around here somewhere that I've come across before at some time? " Bill persisted.

"Not likely." Tom knew of no relatives anywhere, which suited him.

The clerk, not getting any response, changed the subject. "Your room's upstairs . . . No.13. It's the room we keep ready for unexpected visitors. The bathroom's at the end of the hall. I see you have no luggage with you. No problem . . . you'll find clothes you can use in the cupboard in your room. A man who departed in a hurry at this time four years ago left them behind. If you wish, you can get food in the dining room, or, if you prefer, the bar lounge. Have a nice evening Mr Allen."

Tom merely nodded. His thoughts were still engulfed by the idea that somewhere there may have been some warning not to enter Rockville that had not registered with him. That suggestion alarmed Tom, because to him, it was a totally unacceptable conclusion. His motto in life was, 'You take what you can, in whatever way you can, because you're a long time dead.' That motto formed a black and white pattern in his brain. That belief would have to be abandoned if he acknowledged premonitions, and anything else even slightly connected with the occult. To him, such things were nothing more than fantasies portrayed in movies that trumped up the bizarre, and delved into what they called, the supernatural . . . life after death. All such topics and their spin-offs were regarded by Tom as 'hocus-pocus' rubbish.

On the other hand, he still wrestled with the difference between the facts as presented by the doctor and his vivid memory of the events, which forced him to enter Rockville. Somehow there were unexplained flaws in his theories. There must be a simple solution to this event, he reasoned, so he did as he always did when a problem arose. He decided to drown it in whiskey and let tomorrow take care of itself.

On entering his room he quickly moved to the mirror to inspect the damage to his face. Surprisingly he found the scratch marks had faded considerably and there were no marks on his stomach. *Strange, but I mustn't have been seeing straight.*

He glanced around the room. On the dressing table he found everything a man would require in the way of shaving items, comb, brush, even hair gel, all previously unused. Wishing he had more clothes with him he opened the cupboard doors. He was pleased at the range of clothes hanging there. They were outfits worn in the circle in which Tom moved, not the outdated ones worn by Bill and the doctor. *Time seems to have stood still for them. It's strange though that someone left his clothes behind, even if he was in a big hurry to leave.*

After finishing his shower, Tom went back to the wardrobe. Although loath to wearing another's clothes, he knew he had no alternative. His clothes needed to be discarded. *Perhaps the clerk could have them laundered for me in readiness for the morning.* He picked out a suit in his favourite shade of blue, and a shirt and tie to match. To his surprise everything fitted as if custom-made for him.

His final act before he left the room was to gulp down four of the strong pain-killing tablets the doctor had given him. *Four are twice as good as two surely.*

He felt refreshed and without any pain – a fact he credited to the tablets. He retraced his steps to the lobby. From there he followed the sign directing residents to the public and private bars.

CHAPTER 3

Thomas Allen decides to help.

Tom pushed open the swinging half-doors. *I feel I'm in some early Australian bush film. There's something unreal about it.* He paused to soak up what was universal throughout the world – the sweet acrid aroma of fermented hops mingling with the smell from burning cigarettes. It was something only a drinker who frequented pubs regularly would understand. These were the ones he usually sought to befriend. In so doing he added to his list of clients. He would join them in drinks as they journeyed into oblivion, after boasting of past glories and swapping stories of conquests, real or exaggerated. In those precious hours, he and his new friends would become like denizens of an oasis, safe from strangers. They could finish up towards the end of the night punching each other silly, but as long as there was a drop of whiskey left in the bottle, the bond created, remained intact. On the morning following, Tom would check the names of prospective clients written in his address book during the previous night's frolics.

Standing at the entrance his eyes scanned those who occupied the bar area. He then swept his gaze over the people in the lounge. Tom was searching for any obviously well off folk with whom it might be worth making contact. Tonight he saw only working-class people, and a few elderly gentlemen in dusty identical overalls. It gave him a flash of nervousness and curiosity combined.

Tom drifted over to the elaborate bar crafted from Huon pine. He planned a chat to the barman. They always gave him a run-down on the local area and its inhabitants. He lowered himself onto a stool, and rested his arms on the counter. The bartender, glancing in his direction, moved to front him.

"What would you like sir?'

Tom noticed a badge on his apron bore the word 'Harry'. "Whiskey please, Harry," he ordered. The bartender was quick. Within seconds Tom was slowly raising his glass to the light to admire its golden sheen. He pressed the glass edge to his lips. As the elixir slid down his throat, Tom could feel the alcohol warming him throughout his body.

The events of the day no longer depressed him – washed out of his system by the first flood of alcohol. His wall of defence never allowed him exposure to any form of vulnerability for long. He had learned that, after consuming enough alcohol, he could enjoy the experience of being at one with the rest of the human race, minus any nagging doubts. He rarely suffered a hangover, for immunity had developed long ago. He could wallow in his 'pastime', without it affecting his ability to operate fully the next day.

Another customer arrived at the bar. Slowly Tom's eyes rolled around to see if the person who had joined him could be a likely new customer. He noted a grey overall-clad older man. *No chance of a sale with this one.* Before Tom turned away he noticed that the man was taking an unusual interest in the star shaped birthmark on his arm. It had become exposed when Tom reached out to hand Harry the money for his drink.

The newcomer interrupted Tom's thoughts. "Evenin' mister," grinned the toothless old fellow. "You've missed the send-off. The parson's gone." Tom ignored him, but the man continued. "I see you're knocking down ya drink as if there's no tomorrow."

Tom remained unmoving, but there was a tingle now in his spine. The old man watched him, waiting for an answer. He had not long to wait.

"Maybe there'll be no tomorrow, but what makes that any of your business?" Tom replied bluntly, turning his head back to gaze soulfully at his now empty glass.

The old fellow was not discouraged. "I want to know one thing, sonny. How long is ya stayin' in town?" There was an underlying determination in his voice that demanded a response

"Leaving first thing in the morning, if it's any of your business," Tom replied hoping to get rid of him.

"You're full of spirit ain't ya son?" The man grinned, showing his naked gums. He moved closer. Tom could smell the alcohol on his breath and turned his face away. He hoped this stranger would get his order and leave. Normally loving company, this time he felt reluctant to become involved. He wanted to be certain no more affluent-looking and therefore potential customers presented themselves.

The stranger turned away, to wink at the bartender. "Three of the same Harry."

Coins were tossed on to the bar, which preceded the scraping of a tray as the bartender slid it along the counter. It stopped in front of the oldish man who clasped each end with his callused hands. He hesitated before moving away.

"Got any relatives in this 'ere town? You sure look like somebody we seen, but not any more, not any more."

"Pretty nosey aren't you?" Tom remarked, and then added sarcastically, "For your information, I wouldn't be drinking alone if I did . . . would I?"

"Then come and join me and me mates at that table under the window. We meet here regular like. It ain't healthy for a man to be drinkin' alone, let alone get drunk on 'is own. By the way, me name's Jack."

Tom gave a quick sweep of the almost empty bar. *Why not?* He slowly detached himself from the bar stool and followed Jack. Perhaps his usual happy drinking disposition would return with company. *If it also adds to my pay packet, okay, but I think I'll miss out with this lot. But I must find out the address of that Lord the doctor mentioned. He'd be a better prospect.*

With the usual formalities over, Tom settled in as he had with others in the past. It did not surprise him that these old timers matched him glass for glass. He became engrossed in their tall tales, which caused much laughter to ring out.

Jack, sitting opposite Tom, suddenly lurched to his feet. In the process he upturned his empty glass while signalling the barmen that he wanted a refill. Still standing, he leaned across the table, to more closely peer out through the large plate glass window. He pointed with a thin wobbly bony finger at the town's low mountain, now made visible by a rising moon.

"The Manor House . . . up there," he whispered – his glassy eyes transfixed on the mountain. "The evil ones, Lord Westley and his missus won't leave. They won't stay where they belong."

Jack's two friends, with sudden movement, raised their hands to restrain him. One said angrily, "Ya said enough Jack. Stop rambling on. The stranger'll think you're out of ya mind."

Tom watched as if he was looking on from a distance, but his curiosity, originally aroused by the doctor, was re-ignited. He wanted to know more. He had not seen anything like a Manor House, only ruins, during his walk from the main road.

"Where's this Manor house you mentioned?" he enquired, his business sense astute as ever. To him 'Manor' spelt 'money' through sales and therefore commission. No one replied.

"I'm frightened," Jack suddenly cried out in a shaking voice, causing his chest to rise and fall rapidly. His breathing gasped out fear as his eyes swept from one fellow drinker to another. The other men again fixed their gaze on him. For a couple of seconds, the atmosphere was thick and heavy. Tom's military trained mind began to stir his sixth sense . . . a foreboding of disaster. It caused him to question once again, whether there was something not right about this town, but he could not put his finger on what disturbed him.

Tom now felt he was living in some past decade as he watched these old-timers in their out-dated clothes, drinking in a hotel that would probably be pulled down and rebuilt somewhere else. He assumed that the old-fashioned look of both town and people was a tourist gimmick. To block out the still uneasy feeling, he forced a smile, trying to bring back the shattered camaraderie. "I'll buy another round of drinks." Tom announced. He raised his hand to attract the waiter.

After two more rounds the little party was back to its previous jovial revelry. Tom now saw an opening to inquire further about the Manor.

Jack had become deep in some private conversation with Paul, so Tom spoke in a muted voice to the quiet man next to him. "I'd like to ask you something. Why did Jack go crazy, yelling about a Manor House?"

Charlie's big round expressionless eyes glued on to Tom's as his whole body swayed back and forth in his chair. Soundless seconds slowly pursued each other through conscious time. Tom was becoming uncertain whether this man would answer as his tight lips and bitter expression remained unchanged. Without any movement of his own body or face muscles Tom waited. He also knew how to play psychological games.

Charlie released his lock on Tom's eyes. He looked around at his friends as if making certain they were fully absorbed in their own conversation, and would not hear what he said. He then shuffled his chair closer to Tom's before he spoke.

"I'll tell you this much. Up on top of that flamin' mountain is Lord Flurice Westley and Lady Phoebe's Manor House. They're English snobs. He's a Lord, like Lord of the Manor stuff they have in England. Here, he sees himself as a god. He may be a Lord, but this Lord's from hell, and a witch is what I call her. He rules this place, and us, ever since he inherited the town and the quarries when his uncle conked out. He's . . ."

"Can you hold on a minute?" Tom interrupted. "What's all this got to do with Jack being so scared?"

"I'm getting to that. Jack used to work for him – a stable hand he was." His voice heightened in bitterness. "Lord Westley's favourite thing is to take 'is horse and dogs for a run. One Sunday Westley told Jack he wasn't riding, but Jack got the horse ready in case he changed his mind, but he left the saddle loose. When he went outside to attend to a second horse, Westley arrived. He quickly mounted his horse before Jack could tell him about the saddle. It slipped. Westley landed on 'is back. When he gets up, he picked up 'is stock whip, walks over to Jack and whipped him to within an inch of 'is life. He added a kick or two for good measure. After he'd tired 'isself out, he walked away, calm as you like, like he'd been punishing one of 'is dogs. Jack's never been the same since."

Tom listened, absorbed in the man's story of a hate no better expressed than by the force of Jack's anger.

"How could anyone get away with that?" Tom queried softly, half to himself.

Not to be diverted the man continued. His voice became more intense with emotion as he relived the past. "Westley blamed Jack, but it wasn't 'is fault. Jack was four months in hospital. Now, he's off 'is head at times."

Tom followed the man's glance towards Jack, who was still engrossed in conversation with his friend, and continued, "Whenever he comes in here to have a few drinks, he sits where he can stare up at the mountain where the Manor is, and . . ."

"What did the police do about it?" interrupted Tom.

"Oh, the cops come all right," the storyteller replied, while twisting his mouth with distaste. "But as usual, nobody saw nothin. The truth is, as long as everyone around here's 'fraid of the Westleys, he stays master and we stay 'is slaves. He gets away with murder. He gives the orders and we do what we're told. He's the lord of everything and everyone, and I think he always will be. To make matters worse, there's a lost kid running around out there. If the parson hadn't left today he'd not be lost. Poor kid . . . if Westley gets a hold of 'im . . ." He trailed off as he became aware that his friends had stopped conversing amongst themselves.

The mummer of voices increased within the lounge area. Tom looked towards the entrance to see single people and whole families drifting into the hotel. Adults sat on chairs, even tables, while children squatted on the floor. Tom peered at the new arrivals through an alcoholic blur. He addressed the barmen who had arrived with his order. "What's going on?"

"Another meeting's been called. The first was to farewell the parson. After the parson left, people realized Joseph was missing. They've come back to organize a search party for the kid. He 'ain't 'round town anywhere I'm told. The whole town'll be here, except of course Reverend Anderson. He's in the process of saying goodbye to his wife privately, before his transport arrives to take him to another town. He's been transferred. That poor kid was like a son to the Andersons. Of course, Lord and Lady Westley won't be here."

This'll be a good opportunity to sum up more locals for new business, and find out more about the Westleys. Tom raised his hand towards the barman. "Harry, bring us another round after this one. Just keep 'em coming." Tom demanded, but the barman did not appear to hear him. He kept walking towards the people still straggling in. "Anyone still out there lookin' for the kid?" he yelled above the babble of voices.

"No." The reply sounded from someone in the crowd. "We've looked just about everywhere, except up on the mountain. We want someone to go there and search, although everyone knows how dangerous and spooky that is. Joseph is not likely to be on the mountain though. He's scared of the Westleys. We want to find a few volunteers to go up, just to make sure, and . ." The voice became silent, and the barman moved away.

The bar and adjacent lounge were becoming filled almost to capacity. Like small towns everywhere in the bush, all the inhabitants supported each other in any crisis that arose. A new waiter began assisting Harry to serve the many thirsty new arrivals. Impatient now, Tom rose unsteadily to his feet and scraped back his chair to confront Harry who had returned to his position behind the bar. Tom wanted an explanation as to why the next ordered round had not yet been forthcoming.

I'm squinting, and I'm unsteady on my feet. I've never been like this before. Was there something in the whiskey, or maybe those tablets shouldn't be taken with alcohol. Perhaps I should go and get some eats. I'll do that after the next drink. Tom sucked in a few deep breaths before approaching the bar. Once there Tom supported himself by propping himself up against the counter, fearful he would keel over. Harry was serving someone at the other end of the bar area, so Tom slapped his open hands firmly down on the polished top to get Harry's attention.

Harry turned at the sound and walked over to Tom.

"Another round I said, Harry."

"I'm sorry but the bar's closed to you as it's obvious you've had enough to drink." The barman's tone was stern. "You'll be off your feet any minute now. Perhaps you'd better leave before that happens." His tone changed to enticing as he continued. "There's a town meeting about to begin, to formulate plans for a further search for a lost boy. You'd be bored sir."

Tom stood his ground, defiantly glaring at Harry.

"Would you like someone to escort you back to your room?" The barmen spoke with practiced politeness.

Tom looked around the room. He realized he was far out-numbered. In military style, he decided it was time to retreat. "Okay mate, have it your way. I'm leaving!" He accompanied his outburst with the thumping of his fist on the counter, before moving away.

Occupied chairs now blocked the side door into the hallway, so aiming his body at the front door, he zigzagged across the room, trying not to trip over children lolling about.

Outside, the wind had not eased. If anything, it was stronger. Standing with legs apart for balance, Tom leaned against a nearby post and looked scornfully back at the hotel. *They're a bunch of amateurs in there. With my army training I could have organized a proper search for the kid . . . no sweat. But it's their loss.*

Tom's thinking continued in that vein, as he began to study the terrain, or as much as he could make out in the dim light. He concluded that, with its one main street and a few side streets, plus some scattered farms around the area, there was hardly anywhere left for them to search. *The town and the beach'd be the first places they'd have concentrated on. The only place left a boy would be likely to hide, would be in those ruins I spotted on top of the cliff. Maybe he's visiting the Manor House Jack reckons is up there. Although what that drunk says about the Westleys being tyrants should be taken with a grain of salt.*

"On second thought I might even look for him myself," Tom mumbled. "I'll show them. I'll find the kid. Should be good for getting their business." Tom had been taught that it was always an excellent policy, as well as shrewd business sense, to create a standing of good repute in any community. Besides, he had nothing better to do. Sleep could wait.

Manor House! Here I come.

Tom walked unsteadily towards the base of the mountain, while inside the Manor House, bloodthirsty Lord Westley and his equally evil wife, gleefully waited for their visitor – an Allen who carried the Mark of the Victim.

CHAPTER 4

Tomas Allen's trek to find the Manor House

'A PATH to the top of the mountain should not be hard to locate,' surmised Tom as he walked on. He felt confident that the streetlights would reveal the way. However, much to his annoyance, they petered out at the end of the park that separated the hotel grounds from the rocky outcrop and the cove. He halted. Wrapped now in complete darkness he became disorientated, perplexed. Tom's better judgement told him to return to the hotel. As he hesitated, the newly risen full moon appeared. It dodged the wind-driven clouds, to light up a set of stone steps a short distant from where he was standing. He pulled out the small torch attached to his hotel room key and flicked it on. Focusing its light on the steps ahead, he began to climb.

The worst effects from his drinking spree were wearing off and the cool night breeze began to sharpen his wits. His legs felt strong and his gait was steady, although he halted to catch his breath when the steps joined a wide path cut into the side of the cliff. The path meandered up the remaining distance to the top. From here onwards he was forced at times to brush aside irritating overgrown vegetation and wayward branches that were almost obstructing his forward movement.

On reaching the summit Tom stepped on to level ground. His body began to ache. He remembered the pain-killing tablets. He pulled the bottle from his pocket and unscrewed the cap. He hesitated for a moment trying to remember how many the doctor had told him to take. He shrugged and emptied the remaining tablets into his mouth and tossed away the bottle. He wished he had something to drink. *There must be a tap somewhere around here.*

He walked on, towards shrubbery. Reaching it, he pushed aside a drooping tree branch, to stare in surprise at the double-sided gates that confronted him. A family crest was woven into their iron construction. The name 'Westley' was scrolled in coloured enamel in the centre of each section.

In the fickle moonlight Tom peered through the iron lacework. Wide-eyed with astonishment, he viewed a magnificent mansion, nestled in all its architectural beauty within a manicured garden. Peeked gables towered above brick walls – many plastered with white stucco – traversed by narrow brown-trimmed slats in decorative patterns. A well-lit pillared arc graced the impressive entrance, where twin lights spilt golden sheen over a large double oak door. *I never thought I'd see a manor house like this outside the U.K. The Westleys must be worth millions. This'll be better than looking for a kid in some old ruins.*

Tom straightened his tie and brushed imaginary fluff from his coat. He smoothed back his hair with both hands before striding with confidence through the unlocked gate. He followed a cobblestone pathway that divided the lavish gardens. It snaked its way towards the glowing entrance area.

Keeping close to the side of the building, Tom had almost reached a large open window from which bright light escaped, when he heard the sound of a woman's voice. He slowed his pace and listened intently. It came again. It was the same sound, that of a woman's voice, but this time was followed by bell-like laughter. Instantly

Tom flicked off his torch. He padded to the window and peered inside.

'Wow!' He gulped as he watched a beautiful woman and her male companion in a close embrace. They kissed, long and ardently. Tom, his tongue moistening his bottom lip, forced his eyes to stay wide open, fearful he might miss something. He expected to see the couple draw closer, but instead, the beautiful young woman stepped to one side of her companion. She glanced out through the window, and directly at him.

The moon, unconcerned with human foibles, momentarily scattered its light over the scene. It reflected on Tom's wide-eyed and reddening face. *Damn!* He expected to hear a scream ring out from those moist red lips. Instead, she gave him the gentlest of smiles. Before a warning to move away registered in Tom's brain, their eyes linked together for an erotic moment in time, causing Tom's nerves to shoot hot sparks of desire throughout his body.

Her partner turned slightly towards the window. A reflex action caused Tom to double up, to be out of sight. He lowered himself further as the moon threatened to reappear. He waited, stone-like. When no one appeared at the window and no angry male voice exploded upon his ears he began to creep away.

Almost completely past the window, he heard a short hiss from behind him. He looked back. The lady was leaning out of the window smiling coyly at him. Her body glistened beneath the sheer transparency of her gown. With the subdued light of the room behind her, together with the afterglow from the moonlit garden, an aura was created, highlighting her marble textured face with its bewitching eyes and tantalising smile. Her full breasts rose and fell, threatening to force themselves from their lacy confinement. Tom gasped. Details of the rest of her body were what men of Tom's temperament fantasised about. His heavy outgoing breath caused him to emit a low whistle. He tensed with fear at the sound, but she smiled more widely, showing teeth white and perfectly matched. Words formed, and came floating on gossamer wings from soft dewy lips that pouted seductively, sending Tom's mouth dry and his heart pounding against his ribs. He was bewitched. Dismissing the obvious – that she was with another man – what he wanted to do was to reach out and touch her.

She half smiled as she spoke softly. "I know you've been watching me. I could see you liked what you saw. It gives me pleasure to be admired. Do you wish to come inside and meet me?"

Tom's body began to respond with a burning desire to clutch her to him. "Yes," he heard himself foolishly mumbling.

"I will open the door for you."

She had invited him in – the most beautiful woman he had ever seen. He strode towards the front door. As he was nearing the entrance Tom froze. Someone, or something, was following him. He stepped into the deeper shadows, and waited.

A young boy stepped out of the dark shelter of the bushes opposite. *A kid . . . no problem.* "Do you live here?" Tom asked. The boy remained silent. "Well? Or are you the kid they're looking for?"

"I suppose I am."

"Well, you're wanted in town. Get going, on the double." Tom snapped the command at him, and then added. "I'd take you home myself but I've something more interesting to do."

The boy did not move. "I can't leave, sir."

"Oh, yes you can . . . now go," Tom argued.

The boy did not react to the command but continued. "I have to tell you something . . . a story. It's about the Westleys. Please listen Tom Allen," he begged.

He knows my name. Must have been nosing around the hotel. But I've no time to waste. He felt moments were now being lost while a present-day 'Aphrodite' was waiting. "I'm not interested in your story kid," he yelled, impatient at this delay. "Off you go . . . back to town."

"Please, you don't understand."

"Listen kid, I don't have time to understand. I take things as I find them, and at this moment you're supposed to be lost, so get back home. As for listening to some kid's story, forget it. Go tell it to your parents. Now get out of my way." Tom was now devoid of any interest in reuniting a lost boy with his family.

The boy backed away. "Please don't go in there," pleaded the boy. "Come away, please."

"For the last time, get!" Tom attempted to push the boy away, but he had stepped out of reach. "Why don't you just go home?" He cast the words back as he walked away. "You're old enough to find your own way down. Now go, before I catch you and belt you across the ears."

"Please . . . don't go in there. You must go away. The Lord of the Manor is a bad man. He's a . . . "

Tom cut him off. "What would a kid like you know? Now . . off." Tom made a swing with his fist to hit the lad, but the boy was too quick and dissolved back into the surrounding blackness.

To hell with him! Tom moved on. He had almost reached the front steps when a shadowy image emerged from the darkness to stand between him and the steps. For an instant he tensed his muscles ready for a fight, but it was the boy again. Now red-faced with anger, Tom tried to grab him by the scuff of the neck but the boy danced out of range.

"For the last time, get lost kid, because the next time I decide to hit you it won't be across the ears."

"Please, Mr Allen sir. There's bad people in there."

"No kid, you're wrong. Pleasure's waiting for me in there." He skirted around the boy and mounted the steps fronting the porch. At the door his hand was about to lift the brass knocker when it opened wide. The beautiful lady was framed in the doorway. Tom's eyes soaked up her radiance. He could have remained where he was and drunk in her alluring presence forever, but the spell-bubble he was in, burst when she raised a small pink hand. She curled her fingers, with their long, blood red nails, upward, enticing him to make haste and enter. Tom Allen knew an invitation when he saw one. He was only too happy to oblige. He had accepted similar invitations in other places over the years, but never from high society women. He wondered what the cost would be. He knew there was always a price to pay.

Her companion appeared from behind the lady. A tall bony man, whose body was balanced on long thin legs, faced Tom. Chalk-white transparent skin was stretched tightly over his cheekbones. His hair was receding at the temples.

He wore black, which accentuated the whiteness of his skin. His obsidian eyes were sunken, and overshadowed by prominent bushy black eyebrows. *What does she see in him?* The pin-sized pupils seemed to prod Tom's soul as the man lifted his chin in a condescending manner. Tom's first instinct was to retreat hastily out through the door and disappear into the night. Instead, he made the gross mistake of standing his ground.

The woman stepped to one side. She retained a shy smile while looking at Tom with the eyes of a spider watching its prey. A shiver travelled the length of his spine – a warning of danger. It was never wrong. But he decided that his body would not object to being devoured by this bewitching predator. Tom regained his composure, but the nerve in his face twitched again. Perhaps *I should retreat now. Maybe that boy was right.* He analysed his chances of getting out of the house if need be, realising that no one knew he was up on the mountain.

Before he could move, the suave, immaculately dressed man spoke with a strong English accent. "Good evening Thomas Allen." His friendly manner helped dispel the anxiety in Tom. *But how does he know my name? The boy does too.*

"Were you troubled by Joseph? He's always hanging around trying to make trouble. He's insane, the poor boy."

Tom's guard was now completely down. *Is the man implying I would listen to a kid*? He felt a rush of anger. His voice rose as he spoke. "Why should I waste time listening to some kid who's sneaking 'round in the dark wanting to tell me some story? I told him to shut up and go home."

The man smiled disarmingly, and to Tom's utter amazement, walked towards him with outstretched arms. He gripped Tom's shoulders as if greeting an old friend after a long absence. It was almost a hug. Surprised, Tom moved away. This sudden friendship on the man's part made him nervous, knowing he had spied on them through the window. But, the man seemed so calm, Tom decided that nothing would upset this man's equilibrium.

"Forgive my manners. We have not yet been properly introduced. I am Lord Flurice Henry Argyle Westley, and this is my lovely wife, Lady Phoebe." *Wife! This place is a laugh a minute.* "Thomas, or may I call you Tom? You have permission to call us by our first names."

Tom found himself unwittingly returning the man's smile. "All my friends call me Tom."

"Friend Tom, you are most welcome in our humble home. It is our great pleasure to be your hosts for the evening." He turned side-on, and with a sweep of his hand embraced the inside of the home.

Tom felt overwhelmed. *So this is the infamous Lord and Lady Westley. I'm surprised by their warm welcome. Maybe they're just a bit kinky in some way.* Judging from films Tom had seen, Lord Westley would fit the description of a gentleman born to the English upper class. *Jack's friend certainly got his story wrong. Just maybe, the town's people are jealous of the life-style the Westleys enjoy.* Tom told himself it was an honour to be standing before a member of the sophisticated English elite, who happened to have a fascinatingly beautiful wife. In her presence he would happily spend large amounts of time.

While Lord Westley was commenting on several of his artefacts Tom allowed his eyes to scan Lady Phoebe's figure. It seemed to glow like a precious diamond through the sheer transparent material of her robe. He quickly dropped his eyes when Lord Westley twisted his tall frame back to speak to his wife.

"Dearest Lady, as we have a guest this evening, please put on something more appropriate, and join us." Lady Phoebe smiled enticingly at Tom as she left them.

"Tom, I do apologise for my wife's attire. Come, we will retire to the lounge. No . . . the library would be more congenial." Westley lightly touched Tom's elbow, and indicated the way with a nod towards a large room opening out from the lounge, now visible beyond a carved cedar archway. Tom walked beside him. He was again feeling nervous at this sudden friendship on Lord Westley's part; knowing he had once again revealed his obvious feelings of desire for his wife.

As Lord Westley continued to walk in the direction of the library, Tom's thoughts became distracted by his surroundings. He had given little attention to the foyer when he entered. His eyes had been riveted on Phoebe. Now, as he followed Westley through the main room, the grandeur of architecture displayed its true worth. The floor was covered with thick carpet, patterned with the Westley family-crest. The pile reached halfway up the sides of his shoes as Tom walked soundlessly across it. A gold fabric lounge with scattered cushions invited guests to sink between its arms and relax. Paintings of mean-faced thin-lipped men with beautiful younger women from times past and present, were portrayed around the walls. A flattering portrait of Flurice with his wife had pride of place. Marble figurines, each on its own pedestal filled the gaps between each painting. Above Tom's head hung the largest chandelier he could ever have imagined existed. Dozens of miniature crystal droplets and candle-flame shaped bulbs seemed to jostle one another for space. Tom felt he had walked into another world.

They reached a smaller archway. "The library is more intimate, I always think," spoke Lord Westley as they continued on.

They entered an area dimly lit by dozens of crystal wall lights set in ornate brass fittings. A large oak desk stood in one corner, beneath casement windows. On the right, shelves of books paraded from floor to ceiling. At the far end stood an elaborate bar. Carved into its surface were hand carved snakes, maidens, and gargoyles, entwined and curling across and around each other. The furniture and ornaments were antique, and reeked of inestimable value.

Flurice Westley noticed Tom observing the decor. "Do you approve our choice of furnishings?"

"They're magnificent . . . worth a heap."

"Yes, family heirlooms and all that. But let us continue. That is, if you do not mind joining me for a drink."

"I could do with one . . . thanks," said Tom.

Westley positioned himself behind the bar while Tom stood on the outside. From force of habit he leaned his elbows on it. He began to wonder why Lady Phoebe had not yet joined them.

Tom was beginning to drink his third whiskey when Phoebe seemed to float into the room. She was draped like royalty, from the dainty satin shoes on which a diamond rested on the front of each, to her Victorian style outfit of frilled lace blouse with its plunging neckline. From her tiny waist flowed a full-tiered pure silk skirt. She had a diamond tiara almost invisible in her jungle of black curls.

    Tom's hormones began to dance as she came close to him. He felt he should bow before her as he had seen people do before the royal family in films, but held himself back. Phoebe sidled closer to him. Her fragrance wafted into the inner parts of his being, numbing his brain. His eyes kept drifting down her smooth throat to her semi-exposed breasts. She gracefully raised her hand. Never a romantic man he took her hand in his. With as much grace as he could muster he planted a quick kiss on it. He felt pleased with himself. Phoebe smiled beguilingly at him.

    "It is such a pleasure to have you as our guest Tom," she purred. Flurice nodded in assent. "But come Tom, do be seated . . . here. It's more comfortable." She indicated the padded Queen Anne lounge chair close to the bar. As Tom hoped, she seated herself beside him. With her husband hovering over them, he fought against the lure of Phoebe's warm body now pressed against his side. He swallowed more of his drink while struggling to take part in the conversation that ensued, which was mostly about their life in England.

    Physically and mentally, Tom began to feel the effects of a long and harrowing day. He struggled against the drowsiness sweeping over him. *I feel strange. Whiskey never makes me drowsy. It must have been the doctor's pills, or was my drink laced? What am I thinking? I've probably drunk too much.*

He began to regret having climbed to the top of the mountain, and recoiled at the thought of returning by the same route. He vainly wished he were back in the motel with Madeline. *I'm not going to get to first base with Phoebe, not tonight anyway. I'll come back tomorrow, early, before I leave. Tonight I'll just cement the friendship, although I'm convinced they're eccentric. They're trying to re-capture the grand past they once lived in England.*

A large ornate clock behind the bar chimed fifteen minutes to midnight. Before the final chime sounded, Tom was sure he heard a scream. Perhaps it was from a radio somewhere, or sound sucked up from the town. Then the sound of a voice reached his ears from somewhere outside, shouting, 'Tom Allen, leave!' Tom ignored it, but the words had a profound effect on Westley. He jumped as if struck by an invisible blow. Rage in Westley's snarling face became clear. The depth of twisted odium apparent in his eyes was hate Tom had seen before in army conflicts, when the passion to kill was upon a man. His nerves tensed at the realisation that this man was capable of anything of a foul nature.

CHAPTER 5

Tom faces the deadly truth

Westley moved in sudden stride towards the front door, grabbing a poker from the fireplace as he passed. His knuckles protruded like small rocks as he gripped it firmly. "I'm going to fix that kid once and for all," he snarled.

Tom should have been unconcerned. He told himself he was not personally involved, so when Westley's declaration doused him in what felt like invisible icy pellets, he was surprised.

Lady Phoebe rose and glided to her husband's side. She took his arm and halted his progress. "Flurice, calm yourself, dearest. You know it has never changed things in the past, and possibly never will. It is a shame the boy won't join us. After all, revenge is sweet. I know it would be much more satisfying to have him present, but do not forget we have our new guest. Another Allen is here to entertain us."

Westley hesitated, but Tom could see cold fury still burning in his eyes. His features had tightened, distorting his face. It had turned into a Halloween mask. Glancing at Phobe's hand resting on his arm, Westley began to relax. His grip on the poker loosened. His face reverted back to a mocking expression, and Phoebe's hand dropped to her side. Discarding his previous mannerism, he left her to walk back out through the archway. He adopted a silky tone of voice, which was almost cajoling as Tom heard him pull open the front door and say.

"Come in dear boy. I've got a Tom Allen here for you to chat to, but for only a minute or two of course. Wouldn't you like to join us? I'm being nicey nicey. Come and see how the Lord of the Manor treats his special guests, but then you know already. It's a shame you're not in here with us to witness the entertainment."

There was only silence from outside. Westley's voice suddenly changed to sharp and menacing as he spat out words like sparks from a furnace, at the invisible subject of his spleen. "Even if it takes me all eternity, I will make you regret you ever existed . . . spy! Pervert! Destroyer! For us Westleys, it's an eye for an eye, a tooth for a tooth . .an Allen for an Allen . . . all marked victims!"

Tom was certain he heard sobbing. He did not know why the boy was so despised by the owners of the Manor House. He only knew that he must have done something very drastic to cause Westley to be so angry. He agreed with Westley. *The kid should be home and not annoying people, but I'll keep out of it. It's not my quarrel.* His mind felt foggy. He would have one more drink, and leave before he fell asleep. Once outside he would persuade the boy to go with him, and thus become a hero to the town people.

Westley returned to join Tom. He appeared to read Tom's thoughts, for he quickly poured and handed him another drink. Tom was about to lift the freshly filled glass when his eyes closed involuntarily. He slid to the floor. He momentarily faded out of consciousness.

As his senses returned, Tom had a feeling of impending doom as he lay on the floor in an undignified manner. The Westleys were looking down on him, half-smiling, while two black slobbering dogs, one on each side, pressed their front paws down on his arms. Flurice

Westley's facial expression was what Tom imagined a happy vampire – round staring eyes under thick raised eyebrows, flat nose, and a wide half sneering, half gleeful grin – would look like when he had cornered an unwilling 'blood donor.' As four pairs of hostile eyes stared maliciously at him, he was puzzled as to why his friendly hosts had suddenly turned menacing, and why the dogs? He had not been threatening them in any way.

"Hell! Is this some sort of joke? Or is it some game you're playing?" he demanded as he attempted to rise. Warning growls came from deep within the dogs' throats. Their lips began to peel upward, exposing their fangs. Their yellow-streaked eyes, now close to his face, held him again motionless. He tried to suppress the rising fear as his brain endeavoured to work out the best possible way out of his predicament.

Flurice Westley gave a satisfied sneer. "Mr Thomas Allen, my advice to you is not to move. These dogs are trained to kill. Any sudden movement and they will rip you apart."

Tom knew he should not take his eyes off the dogs. They were poised, ready for action as saliva began to drool from their mouths. Their breaths were hot and putrid. They waited for a command from their owners. Tom began to feel the first beads of cold sweat oozing from every pore of his body. "Call your bloody dogs off, Westley," Tom yelled. "Why the hell are you doing this?"

"Revenge, dear boy, revenge! An Allen has caused me more problems than you could possibly imagine. I had the misfortune to have one cross my path here in Rockville, to my detriment. Like you, he had the Allen star shaped birthmark." *How does he know that?*

"We regret ever coming to this cultural wilderness, where I have found myself surrounded by the incompetent lower classes who cannot speak the King's English, or should I now say Queen's, correctly. How Uncle Worsley worshipped this country and started the mines here at Rockville is incomprehensible to me. I find it so degrading, although I have become accustomed to being the lord of all I survey. I am the controller of all lives, and deaths, hereabouts." He raised his voice. "I am the lord of all I survey. I am Lord Flurice Henry Argyle Westley." He gave a quick glance towards his wife. "Do you agree, dearest?" His wife smiled and nodded.

"But I digress. Suffice to say that anyone who spies on us, crosses us, or does us damage, comes to a nasty end. It is a vow I swore to keep after what that other Allen did. If I do not take revenge I would be dishonouring the family name. Our glorious family history is built on revenge." He paused for a moment in thought. "I do wish the boy would come inside. He's a backward oaf, but having him present would add a certain zest to the proceedings. You see Tom, I owe the kid, and I mean to settle that score in full. As I said, I am the lord, and no-one can say unto a lord, 'what doesn't thou?" He laughed a high-pitched, nerve-racking laugh.

Tom did not comprehend what Westley was talking about. *He's a raving lunatic.* Now he fully understood why the town's people hated him. How the boy came into the picture, he could not even hazard a guess. Nothing made sense to Tom. Could he reason with this maniac? He would try, if only to gain time.

"Be reasonable," Tom begged. "It was an accident. I wasn't perving. I just happened to be passing the window. You shouldn't have left it open. Call off the dogs and let me up. I'll leave Rockville and never mention anything to anyone."

Tom tried to make another effort to get to his feet, but the dogs' growls aborted the movement. Befuddled, and with anger increasing, he wanted to tell Westley it was his wife who had invited him in, but he did not risk further inflaming Westley's temper. Instead he yelled, "You were so pally when we first met."

Westley ignored him. "Mr. Allen, please look at me, not at the dogs, so I may pass sentence."

"Sentence . . . what sentence?"

"You are sentenced by the members of this court, Lady Phoebe and myself, to be tried for spying, and anything else I might think of. Is that a unanimous decision my dear?"

Tom turned to look directly at Phoebe, refusing to believe she was playing any part in this madness. He was horrified by her expression. The beautiful Lady Phoebe had acquired a gleeful look of anticipation. No help would come from that source. Tom's body shuddered with shock waves of realisation as Phoebe drew from the folds of her skirt, a long thin edged knife.

"Yes, my Lord . . . anyone with the Allen birthmark, which he has, is guilty."

How did she know that? It's been covered the whole time.

"How perceptive of you my dear. So, regrettably Thomas Allen," Westley continued. "You leave me no choice. From the evidence presented here, there is but one verdict I can pass. It's guilty'. You are sentenced to death."

Tom knew he must act, even though he realised that the odds were stacked against him. *I've had enough* of this English Pom's grandstanding – *dogs or no dogs.* He tried to scramble to his feet. Westley clicked his fingers. The dogs attacked. One gripped Tom's throat, although no teeth pierced his skin. The second dog straddled the rest of his body, pinning him down. Still struggling, Tom freed one arm. Westley pinned it to the floor with his foot. Horrified, and powerless, he watched Phoebe pass the knife to her husband.

Westley paused with it held a few inches from Tom's face. "Because I am a gentleman, as well as the learned judge at this trial, you are granted permission to say some last words before you die." He spoke with a twisted smile on his distorted face. His slanted eyes bulged beside the hooked nose, and the sneering smile revealed long crooked teeth. His black coat tails floated backward resembling a cloak as he began to sway back and forth. Tom was reminded of a 'demon from hell' he had once seen at the local showground. That creature jumped out from dark hidden places to frighten customers who paid to travel through a darkened tunnel.

The spirit of courage now stirred within Tom. It spoke to him in his hour of need. During the Vietnam War, he had often wondered why, when badly wounded, he had not met death while many of his buddies had perished. *My doctor once told me I'd never live to old age. But I didn't think it'd all end this way.*

Taking a deep breath to quell the feeling of fear and horror rising within him, Tom forced a tone of contempt. He remembered reading in a manual once, 'Revenge may be sweet, but it will turn to bitter acid when another stronger than you comes along and challenges you. That's the law of the jungle. Eventually good will triumph over evil." He had never before fully believed good always won, but then his country was always on the winning side when engaged in any military enterprise, so it must be true. *That's proof enough.* He then added. "There's no escape for the two of you. You both'll burn in hell forever."

The last sentence impacted on Westley. For a fleeting moment Tom saw pure fear creep like a dark red stain across Westley's eyes, but within seconds he had mastered himself, raising his arm, ready to plunge the knife into Tom.

Suddenly mesmerised, like a cobra before a mongoose Tom felt strangely calm, accepting his destiny. He became an outside onlooker as Westley's knife began to descend. *Like my fallen mates I'll accept my fate with dignity.* He did not feel the first stab that pierced his eye.

Westley stepped aside to allow Phoebe to take his place. She raised a smaller knife she had drawn from amongst her clothing. Tom did not feel the slicing carried out by her on his lower body in the shape of a star. He floated above the gruesome scene until darkness blotted out all awareness.

With Tom's lifeblood dripping off the knife, Westley threw back his head and laughed. His chilling, penetrating laughter echoed throughout the house. It leapt outside, through windows and walls, to be trapped within the wind currents that dumped this burden of evil as they whirled through the town.

The clock chimed midnight. The building began to shake as if by an earth tremor. The wind captured the sound, together with a single childish scream. Diabolic laughter followed. It streamed outwards to overrun the surrounding land, as Westley dragged Tom's body to the edge of the cliff. He gave it a shove and it rolled over the jagged edges to land in the high grass covering the ground below.

One by one the lights in the town were switched off. All windows were shut tight long before its frightened inhabitants crawled into bed, to lie, awaiting sleep that eluded them. They had heard screams and laughter on the wind before, and prayed they would never hear it again. Their prayers had not yet been answered. All they wanted was to be at peace, away from the spectre from hell. They prayed for a rescuer, a saviour, hoping that next leap year the burden would be lifted.

CHAPTER 6

Police Superintendent Steven Barnes makes a vow

It was the morning of March 1, 2004. Within the Police Precinct offices on the main street of the small town of Greystone, Chief Superintendent Steve Barnes' day began as usual. A steady flow of routine matters commanded his attention.

That was, until his deputy, Mario Martino, stood at the open door of his office waiting for permission to enter. "Excuse me Sir, but it's urgent," he barked.

His words shattered the orderliness of his Superintendent's methodical work, whose round ruddy face was frowning as his eyes stared out from under his heavy eyebrows. In a gesture of impatience he tossed his pen down upon the piles of papers cluttering his desk. Leaning forward, he sighed as he rested his uniform-clad elbows on the table, resigned to yet another interruption to his busy schedule.

"What's your problem Martino?" His voice was edgy.

The deputy took that to be an invitation to enter. He marched in briskly and stood stiffly, almost at attention. "I wish to report Sir that Officer Grice has radioed in. He found a car abandoned on the side of the road between Greystone and Little Rock. He requests back-up."

"Back-up for an abandoned vehicle on the side of a road? Tell Officer Grice his request is denied."

"Yes Sir."

Martino turned, ready to exit the office but something was twigging in the back of his Chief's mind.

"Wait!" was the command.

His deputy halted, then quickly pivoted to face his senior officer.

"Where exactly is this vehicle?"

"Grice reported its locality as being near the old turn-off to Rockville."

"Near the old road into Rockville?" Barnes echoed.

"Yes Sir."

His Chief automatically glanced at his calendar for confirmation of his suspicions. It read, March 1, 2004, a leap year. *Yesterday, February 29th was the date of previous mysterious deaths in the area.* Barnes pursed his lips. The colour drained from his face. Stress had that effect on him. He began to tap out a steady beat with his nails on the only exposed space on the polished desktop.

"Are you all right Sir?"

"Of course I am. But being near the Rockville turn-off puts a different light on it. Forget that previous instruction. I want you to get out there. Take one of the other officers with you. Report back to me immediately you know something, or find anyone. Before you leave though, get back on the radio and tell Officer Grice I want to speak to him immediately." Martino nodded. "Have you anything else to report?"

"No Sir, but can I ask a question?"

"Well?"

"Sir, so I was right in thinking this matter was urgent. I mean you're obviously concerned. This report of an abandoned vehicle seems to be of greater importance than usual."

The Superintendent's suddenly raised voice startled his junior into silence. "What the hell are you still standing here for? I told you to get Sergeant Grice immediately. Now move it!"

His deputy quickly retreated from this verbal blast.

Superintendent Barnes had reason to be worried. He had been a member of the police force for almost thirty years, and the head of the Greystone precinct for four. He loved his job, and had a good relationship with his men. They were honest, hardworking, and eager to do their jobs well and to survive. He had made it a rule to try to maintain a friendly team environment. Although strict rules of conduct were enforced during working hours, he always treated his men with respect. He understood why Martino had been surprised when he had spoken to him so abruptly. *I'll explain to him later.*

Unknown to his deputy the orderly routine of his Superintendent's working day had been shattered. The old sick feeling, deep in his gut, stirred into life, just as it had after that 'accident' that occurred in the leap year of 2000. That was when a Patrick Allen had been found horribly murdered at Rockville, and he was not the first either. Similar mutilated corpses had been found there in previous leap years, and to date no one had been made accountable.

All reports had been buried in the police archives when no new evidence could be found to warrant further investigation. Any relatives they managed to locate were few, or too distant and not forthcoming. He feared it would be the same this time. He visualized an autopsy report showing the time of death to be around midnight, February 29. Y*esterday – the same date as the previous ones.*

The voice of Martino severed his concentration. "Grice on the line now Sir."

He pressed the button on his board. "Grice . . . good . . . run it past me."

"There's this abandoned car with a flat tyre parked on the side of the coast road between Greystone and Little Rock . . . near the entrance road into Rockville. I believe it's been here since late yesterday. Must be some city bloke. He's got a spare but it doesn't look like he even attempted to change the tyre."

"Well, why do you need back up? Isn't it a simple matter for the tow truck people to handle?" The question was a standard one and Barnes hoped for a simple reply.

"Sir, when I arrived I noticed the driver's side door was partly ajar and the keys still in the ignition. At first I thought the owner might have gone for a short walk, you know, or got a lift into town. I've been calling out, but got nothing back. I waited about fifteen minutes, then I did some more checking." Sergeant Grice paused.

Growing impatient at this gap in the conversation Barnes was abrupt. "Go on Grice. What else have you got?"

"There's what looks like blood stains on the steering wheel cover, and a small amount on the roadside below the driver's door. The ground there's badly scarred. There might have been a struggle of some kind, but I've only found one set of footprints so far. They're from a pair of men's shoes. I traced them as far as the old Rockville turn-off. The marks are clear and deep. They must have been made when the ground was soft from the rain last night."

He was heading towards Rockville? I'm right. The horror's repeating itself.

"When no one appeared, I looked inside the car. I found an unlocked briefcase, full of papers, receipt books, cheques, and some cash. There doesn't seem to be anything stolen. There's no evidence of a disturbance. Oh . . . and there's a phone too. It was on the floor. It's working, so it's a mystery to me why he hadn't rung for help."

Trying to sound casual Barnes asked, "Have you asked the traffic branch to make a search?"

"Yes Chief, but if the car's been stolen we haven't been notified yet."

"Whose name's on the documents?"

Barnes could hear the rustle of papers. His fingers once again drummed in rhythm on the desktop. He wanted to know, yet feared what he might hear. *Why is he taking so long?* "Grice, whose name's on the papers?" he repeated.

The reply came back. "The receipts have Tom Allen stamped on them. The letterheads have Thomas M. Allen at the top,"

The Superintendent's stomach churned when he heard the name 'Allen'. *That was the surname of the last victim. Yes, a Patrick Allen. Where he was from they never found out. All the victims were Allens. There was a John Allen. His family claimed they had no idea why he was in Rockville. Before that, it was James whose relatives were also never located. Is the same killer returning again and again in a four-year cycle? Is it a bizarre coincidence that the victims all have the same surname? Why did they all end up in that same area during the dying days of February and always in a leap year?*

Barnes knew he could not wait in his office for news. He wanted to personally verify the truth. If his suspicion were correct, it would turn out to be another ludicrous, mysterious leap year death. He would accompany his deputy to Rockville. He had to be sure.

"Are you still there Sir?" Grice called loudly, puzzled by the silence on the other end of the line.

"Yes, Grice. Now listen. I want you to stay by the car. I'll be there shortly."

He put a request through to his secretary. He wanted a member of the forensic team, and the paramedics to meet him at the scene. He replaced the phone as he jumped out of his chair. This forced it to wheel back and crash against the wall behind him. He feared his deputy may have left, but on entering the outer office he found Martino pulling on his jacket.

"Hold it Martino. I'll take over from here."

His second-in-command's eyebrows rose in surpris*e. If the Chief is taking over so be it, but I can't think why.*

Barnes scanned his team. They were watching him with rising excitement. The Super's actions suggested something unusual was happening. He moved past the row of desks. "Martino, you're to come with me, and you too Norris."

Martino picked up the telephone with one hand and straightened his cap with the other. "I'll let Grice know we're leaving now, Sir."

"Be snappy about it," boomed Barnes as he hastened towards the exit.

"We're on our way Grice." Martino spoke quickly before dropping the receiver back into its cradle. He hurried to catch up with the Chief who was marching determinedly out the door, followed by Senior Constable Norris.

Barnes' irritability was evident during the drive. He sat, with his body rigid, in the front passenger seat. He clipped orders to the driver. He urged him to speed, and then slow down when he reached well over the speed limit. He ceased when he caught sight of the abandoned car. Norris slowed the police car to a crawl and parked it at the rear of Officer Grice's car, stationed close to the disabled Holden.

The Superintendent was the first to alight. Without a word, he circled the abandoned car several times. He could see that no accident had occurred. The car itself was not damaged. It merely had a flat tyre. However Grice had been correct. There were bloodstains. His three officers waited on tenterhooks. They were curious as to why their Chief had taken such an unprecedented interest in this incident. On such routine matters he had always given his men full rein.

He rejoined his deputy. "Martino, you're to stay here and wait for the forensic people, and the paramedics, or the return of the driver if he does come back. Though I doubt that will happen. The rest of us will inspect the area from here to the base of the Rockville Mountain."

He withdrew his gun before turning to his other officers. "Have your weapons ready and follow me." His men glanced at one another in surprise. Barnes guessed what they were thinking. *Forensic? Paramedics? Guns? There's no body. Has he lost it?*

As they watched, Barnes squeezed the handle of his gun tightly. He was convinced he would find the murdered body of Thomas Allen somewhere in the vicinity of the Rockville Mountain. Perhaps this time the killer may still be around. He and his men would be ready if they did sight him. Given the time lapse, he knew this would be unlikely.

"Are we taking the cars Chief?" The question from Grice interrupted his troubled thoughts.

"No, they stay put. Martino will guard them. We don't want to destroy any ground markings that might help our investigation. Spread out and keep your eyes peeled."

"Apart from tracks, what else are we looking for Sir?"

"A body and anything that moves . . . anything . . . follow me."

The startled expression on their faces almost drew a smile from their Chief. He could read their thoughts. *He's never gone off the rails like this before. A dead body! All we're looking for is a missing driver. A murderer would have grabbed the cash before he ran off.*

Martino had remained poised, catlike, while his Chief spoke. One hand was now resting on the butt of his gun, still in its holster. His eyes were alert and watchful, reflecting his Super's mood. Should anyone other than the driver appear to claim the car, he would be ready.

The group advanced along the main road towards the Rockville intersection. Realising the seriousness of their quest, Grice and Norris, each with a hand resting on their gun holsters, tracked behind their Chief as he turned briskly into Rockville Road. They kept approximately two metres apart while their eyes scanned the ground for evidence of any disturbance on the road surface, then to the bushes for any movement, however slight. They saw nothing of note and heard no sounds, except for the shuffling of their own feet. Otherwise, it was eerily quiet.

When the officers reached the crossroads, they halted. For a few moments they looked around them. Rocks from the old mines, of all shapes and sizes dominated the scene. They stared at Rockville's low mountain now facing them, and blocking their view of the sea. Turning their gaze towards the town itself, they viewed crosses in a cemetery, pointing upwards like so many tall garden stakes, before quickly turning away.

The Superintendent kept treading in a direct line to the base of Rockville Mountain. That was where the corpse had been found four years ago. In the original report it was ascertained that the victim had been murdered on the mountaintop and the body pushed over the cliff. As a thorough search unearthed no clues, the final verdict was 'cause unknown, a possible death by 'misadventure'. No further investigation was carried out, and no explanation given as to how the man reached Rockville and finished up lying dead on the spot where he was found.

Signalling to his men to spread out, they tentatively moved towards the area of tall dry grass on which Barnes was concentrating. He was looking for a body that he hoped he would not find. The men, realizing that their Chief was actually looking for a body, moved forward quickly, stamping through grass and tall weeds with the same intention.

Barnes began to doubt his instincts, until sunrays, deflecting from what he guessed could be a watch face, shot a sliver of light upward from between the weeds. His stomach muscles tightened. He moved closer. At times he struggled to stay upright whenever his shoes got caught in the tangled mass of thick grass. On reaching the spot where he had glimpsed the narrow flicker of light, he reluctantly parted the tall loose brittle stalks. The open, damaged and bloody eyes in the face of a deceased male seemed to stare up at him.

Barnes stayed unmoving while he viewed the lifeless victim. The man's wounds caused him to turn cold at the thought of what he must have endured at the hands of his killer. He involuntarily shivered as he looked from the almost empty eye sockets to the gashes on the stomach region, where knife cuts formed a rough outline of a star. Barnes noticed a birthmark on one of the exposed arms. It was familiar. *That star shaped birthmark is similar to the ones found on the other unfortunate Allens. They all carried the same 'mark of the victim'.* His worst fears had been realised. There was no doubt in his mind that this was Thomas Allen, the owner of the abandoned car.

He beckoned to his officers. They scrambled through the thicket to stand beside him. In shocked silence they stared down at the body. They struggled to accept what they were seeing. Shaking, they turned away with churning stomachs. They had seen accident victims at the hospital or at the morgue, but never anyone mutilated in this manner.

This new death ignited intense repugnance in the Superintendent. This had lingered just below the surface for four years. It had begun when he had stood, viewing the body of Patrick Allen. His mind tried to dispel the visual image, to rid himself of the feeling he was back in the past, looking at the same man. They had the same build, the same complexion, and the same straight blond hair that tended to fall lazily over the forehead. He also possessed a similar birthmark. *Brothers perhaps?* The number of strange coincidences had him perplexed. *Why has the murderer returned to this exact spot, and always at the same time in a leap year to find his victims, all with the same surname . . . Allen. Perhaps there's a vendetta against the Allen family? If so, why didn't they avoid the place?* So many questions, with few, if any, easy answers. At least none that Barnes could discover.

He knelt down beside the corpse. He wanted to examine it more closely, to be certain that the injuries could not possibly be caused solely by a fall. But he knew the forensic people would arrive shortly, so he must not disturb anything. He rose, convinced that this was not caused by an accident. *The killer has to be caught before it happens again.*

Superintendent Barnes silently swore that he would devote all his energies to solving the mystery, and preventing the horror of Rockville from continuing. He sensed the truth was out there somewhere in his precinct, but where? He could not put his finger on anything close to a plausible explanation. *Where to start? For the present it's back to routine checks.*

Breathing deeply, in an effort to calm his inner turmoil, Barnes straightened up. He turned to his two young officers. They were pale but now composed. "Have you anything to report?" inquired Barnes. They announced they had not found anything they could connect to the body. No footprints or trampled grass had been found anywhere near the corpse. They found no trace of blood, or weapons. They waited for further instructions.

No one, decided Barnes, could have entered or left the area without leaving some trace of their presence. At his orders his men would continue scanning the landscape for any missed tell-tale signs, broken trees, fallen rocks, footprints. It was as if someone on wings had descended, carried out their foul deed and departed the same way.

'When you finish in this area, start searching further afield. Check the mountaintop itself first. If you find nothing, cover the rest of this area. Double-check everything and everywhere, including the beach and the cove. Look for any discarded weapons. Check for signs of anything like an occult ritual, especially near the cemetery. After that, visit any homes along the highway near the Rockville Road entrance. Someone might have seen someone entering, or heard something. What we need is answers. Let's see that we get them. Go, and do your job the way you've been trained to do it. We must get positive results."

"Yes Sir," they replied respectfully, intrigued that their Chief's earlier assumption had proved correct. The missing driver was indeed a murder victim.

"Here are the paramedics now Sir," Norris announced.

"There's nothing they can do for this bloke. It's over to the forensic people now. I'll send Deputy Martino down here. He'll be in charge. I want reports on my desk as soon as possible after you return to the station. That's a priority. I want my final report finished as soon as possible."

"Yes Sir."

Barnes walked towards the paramedic and forensic crews as they neared the base of the mountain.

After the initial greeting he told them all he had observed. He requested a report as soon as possible, before trudging back to his car, to return to his office.

Back behind his desk Barnes foraged around for the list of those named in the previous mysterious deaths in Rockville, which he kept in his locked filing cabinet. It confirmed what he already knew. They were all Allens. The first victim was a John, following by James, then Patrick, and now Thomas Allen. As Barnes already knew from previous reports the station had exhausted all possible avenues in their enquiries. No witness, or likely suspect, had been discovered. That was, except for one.

He was Reverend Andrew Anderson, a parson of the Church of Christian Followers. He and his deceased wife had lived in Rockville until he was transferred to Stanholme. He had been seen entering the Rockville Road on at least two occasions. The police had assumed it was for no legitimate reason. The Reverend claimed he came to pray at his wife's grave. He added that he also prayed for the salvation of some young boy who needed all the prayers he could offer up for him.

During the interview the parson insisted, "You'll never arrest anyone. There's more to Rockville than you can ever imagine." He had stood up and placed his right hand on a cross resting on his chest. It was attached to a thick chain encircling his neck. He had spoken in a solemn manner. "The Bible says, 'Revenge is mine, saith the Lord, but another lord from hell returns in February of every leap year to lure in a marked victim, always an 'Allen' family member, to his death. This lord seeks revenge on the Allen family for the actions of a predecessor. This evil lord is named . . ."

The office telephone had suddenly rung, cutting short the interview. His Chief had received the information that Reverend Anderson had a history of admissions to psychiatric institutions following the death of his wife. He was dismissed and his statements discounted.

Barnes never forgot that discussion. Out of curiosity, he had made a search of the station's records. The results were astounding. He learned that two of the previous deaths were put down to possible drowning. It was then concluded, that both had most probably landed on the rocks after a fall from the cliff top when climbing or skylarking. The gorged eye and the cuts on the body were not mentioned in detail.

Now there was another Allen, a Thomas Allen, who had died in Rockville. Photographs confirmed that the star-shaped birthmark on the other bodies was similar to the one on this latest victim, but they had not been considered of importance in the earlier investigations.

Barnes had kept the conversation between the parson and his then Chief alive in his memory. He knew that to believe the murders were the work of an angry lord from another world was to rationalize the occult. Although mentioned briefly in the report it proved unsustainable and was therefore dismissed.

. . . .

At Thomas Allen's funeral, Superintendent Barnes positioned himself at a discreet distance from the group attending the burial service at the Rockville Cemetery. He had been unsuccessful in locating any of

Thomas Allen's next of kin. There was no record in the deceased's belongings of any relatives. Barnes decided that Rockville would be the body's final resting place.

He stood in the speckled shade of several straggly trees, which had been distorted by lashings from strong westerly winds. His eyes closely examined the only mourner paying her last respects. She was a slim tall girl quietly sobbing. She was a Madeline somebody, a barmaid, who claimed she was Thomas Allen's 'defacto'. No other strangers appeared on the scene, and she did not fit the profile of a killer. She stood close to the funeral parlour attendants as they lowered the coffin into the earth.

Although the Chief appeared relaxed, inwardly he was angry and frustrated. He was no closer to arresting anyone. He had stationed Deputy Martino and Officer Grice in a police van some distance away. He chose a spot within viewing distance of the immediate area. Barnes did not believe the murderer would be in attendance, but allowed himself a faint hope that the perpetrator would return to view the finale of his criminal act. If he did, they were ready to take him into custody.

Barnes glanced across the neglected churchyard to where four, already dug, but unfilled, graves, waited to be claimed by those whose names had been engraved on the tombstones. He wondered where they were. All the inscriptions were now faint and faded. They were hardly readable. One name however, was familiar to him. It was Parson Anderson, who Barnes believed was still alive. *Who and where are the other three?* Barnes decided that, if deceased, they must have been buried elsewhere. It was something that only Police Superintendent Barnes seemed interested enough to want to unravel.

A depressed Barnes swallowed his disappointment at his lack of success in finding any clues to the present murder. He had neither a suspect nor a motive. The investigation was fraught with difficulties. The deceased man was a 'loner'. Rockville held many secrets and this death added another puzzling chapter to the mystery.

He resolved to tackle the uphill battle ahead of him with fanatical zeal. He would not cease his self-imposed mission to find the killer. He would start once again, to search for something, anything, that might have been overlooked previously. He may have missed something relevant. If he failed this time, the next leap year of 2008 would be a beacon. It was only four years away. He would be ready.

"Funeral's over Sir. They're starting to leave."

"Thanks Martino. We'll wait for the funeral entourage people to leave Rockville, then it's back to work."

"Do you think we'll ever find out why this fellow was murdered, and who did it?"

"Given time, yes. I'm sure that in time we will. We must." But Barnes' tone lacked conviction. He realised the magnitude of the task before him. *It won't be for want of trying, but, unless we get something to go on soon, or someone starts spilling their guts, it'll be impossible.*

If no leads are forthcoming this time and the perpetrator eludes us, a stakeout in the 2008 leap year is going to be a reality. Now I'm in charge I'll see to that. It would, Barnes felt confident, solve the mystery once and for all

Although I've received an offer to accept a vacant position of lecturer in Stanton, I shall postpone it if at all possible. If not, I'll still continue my connection with the new Superintendent, who will most likely be Mario Martino, and return to Rockville in February 2008. I will never rest content until the case is solved.

BOOK 2

FOUR YEARS HAVE PASSED

IN THE LEAP YEAR OF 2008

THE ROCKVILLE HORROR RETURNS AS

THE LORD OF ALL EVIL WATCHES AND

WAITS FOR ANOTHER MARKED VICTIM.

FROM THE DIARY OF A MARKED VICTIM

GREG ALLEN

WRITTEN WHILE IN THE GRIP OF THE

ROCKVILLE MYSTERY

There comes an important turning point in everyone's life whether they realise it at the time or not.
In the leap year of 2008 mine came in the form of a test of courage in the face of fear, horror, and things unimaginable.

Greg Allen

CHAPTER 7

Another Allen (Gregory) arrives in Rockville.

The journey that unintentionally took me into Rockville began quite innocently.

In February 2008 my Grandmother Audrey Allen died. I, Greg Allen, and my best friend and cousin Mike Mitchell were notified at Queensburg University Campus. This was where we lived and studied . . . me, the Arts . . . Mike, Nuclear Physics. We both enjoyed sports and were accomplished players in the Uni football team. I was also the editor of the University News Magazine. Turning words into stories and articles was a great passion of mine.

At first light we left on our Harley Davidson motorbikes to attend our grandmother's funeral in Stanholme. We did not loiter on the way and arrived well in advance of the proceedings.

During the sad ceremony, as I stood in the church between my distraught parents, I recalled my last visit to my Grandmother. She lay in her hospital bed; a cancer patient. Her body was small and shrunken further by her illness, but she was still mentally alert. On arrival and after planting a swift kiss on her forehead, she smiled up into my face. Taking hold of my hand she said, "I'm so happy you and Mike could come." She hesitated as if in deep thought, before continuing. "You're so like your dear Grandfather, Jonathan. You know we lost him mysteriously. Perhaps you could . . ."

I interrupted her. "Who's Jonathan? His name was Patrick wasn't it?'

"Your Grandfather's full Christian names were Jonathan Patrick. He hated the name Jonathan. He insisted on using his second name, Patrick. He made me promise I wouldn't tell anyone his first name was Jonathan. He used it only for official or legal purposes. As you know, he was last heard from when he stopped at some small beach place. Perhaps one day you'll be able to find where they buried him, and lay a wreath for me on his grave." She stopped speaking. I knew she was trying to hold back the tears.

"I will Grandma, I will." At the time I did not believe that I would be able to keep that promise. No one seemed to know the exact location of his disappearance. But when I spoke those words she brightened up. Her eyes travelled over me as she said, "You remind me of him. You're tall and have the same blue eyes as he did; the same athletic build, the same blond streaks in your hair, and it's just as unruly. He couldn't keep it out of his eyes either."

Her gaze was now resting on my hand, which she still held in hers. Her eyes lingered on the star-shaped birthmark near my wrist. It stood out clearer with the pressure of her grip. "You have the Allen side of the family birthmark. Your cousin Mike doesn't. He takes after my side . . . the Mitchells. Most of us have dark wavy hair. His zest for living makes him the opposite to you. Your more thoughtful ways show in your gentle manner, but he has a cheekiness that I adore. I'm pleased you both get on so well. I love all my grandchildren, but you, my boy, are my favourite." It was the last time I saw her alive.

Mike and I said our farewells to family and friends with sadness, and promises to see each other more often. The funeral reinforced our belief that life was to be lived to the utmost, or perhaps I was also somewhat influenced by Mike with 'drink and be merry' as his motto.

We decided that, having to attend a family funeral, gave us an excuse if we were late back at College. We always wanted to see more of the countryside, so we decided to detour – return home via the coastal strip. We could also put the strength and endurance of our beloved motor bikes to greater tests.

On our way we stopped where we fancied, noted the local 'talent', and sometimes got 'lucky'. We did not stay at any place for long, and usually left after the venue we were socializing at, mostly the local pubs, closed. Sometimes this would be around midnight. This plan allowed us to avoid paying for overnight accommodation. Most nights we parked at a rest area and caught up on some of our lost sleep.

We believed we always knew exactly where we were at any given time. That was until we found ourselves on a coast road halfway between the small towns of Little Rock and Greystone. We had not originally planned to veer so far off the main highway but it seemed we had.

As the early morning sun appeared over the horizon and began to warm our bodies, Mike gestured to me to pull over to the side of the road. When we both stopped he said, "Well mate, you've got us lost." His eyes twinkled. This was a chance for him to rile me – a habit of his, which neither of us took seriously. "At that last stop you must have read the map upside down. You were probably hung over from last night. That was a hoot wasn't it? You lost, but I won $150 at that casino."

"Lucky you." I said, only half listening to what he was saying, as I had begun to scrutinise the area map I always kept in a pouch on my motor bike. "Look." I pointed to a spot marking a turn-off to a small seaside town called Rockville only a few kilometres further on.

"Didn't notice that name before, and it wasn't on any of the signs we've passed."

"I didn't see any sign either and my sight's better." He grinned again, and then added seriously, "I think we should stop for a while. I could do with a nap. Maybe we could stay the night if there's some life in the place."

"Right," I agreed, beginning to feel the need for a break from concentrating on the road for so long. We could also wash the dust from our bodies, and more importantly, take away the dryness from our throats. While there we could also top up our tanks. Although they were a little over half full, the added fuel would mean we would not have to seek out petrol stations for some considerable distance.

After I refolded the map and packed it away, we again sped off. On reaching a Rockville directional sign we turned sharply off the main road and into Rockville Road. Maintaining our speed, we zoomed between trees growing thickly on each side.

We yelled 'Yah Hoo' whenever we almost lost our seating as we bounced up and down over bumps and rocks. The road was uneven and the surface neglected. The area around us looked desolate. I wondered if there really was a town, or just a beach with two or three stores fronting it. What we seemed to be heading towards was a low rocky mountain on which a surrealist structure was eerily silhouetted against the bright, orange sky. Ruins of a large building were perched precariously on this rocky outcrop. As the glow washed over the ruins I could see that parts of the remaining walls stood defiantly erect. Others leaned forward at a drunken angle as if bowing towards the sea in bitter mourning.

I was about to call to Mike to tell him that we were probably entering a ghost town when we approached a

'Welcome to Rockville' sign at a crossroad. It indicated that Rockville town was to the right, and Rockville Mines to the left.

Swinging right, we were happy to see houses appear. They seemed to rise out the morning fog. *The town at last.* The fog was strangely absent as we drew closer to the town proper. Billowing clouds of dust now followed in our wake. Riding parallel to Mike I shouted to him that it was February 29th so being a leap year, we had an extra day to enjoy ourselves, one more than when February ended on the 28th. He shouted back. "At the end of our lives we will have lived longer than the number our years indicated, and that must be a plus." I agreed to that.

As we passed a park, we eased off the throttles on our Harleys, slowing to almost a walking pace as a hotel sign suddenly flickered into life. I had an unsettling feeling about the place. It was too quiet, apart from the sound of a restless sea we could not as yet see. I felt we were being watched – not an unusual pastime in tiny communities where visitors were few. What also appeared unreal was that the usual vivacity of other seaside towns was absent here. I felt that tourists and visitors must be few. Perhaps this was due to that ruin-topped mountain, whose shadow, like a heavy choking hand, had crept over this small town, nestled against its base. I looked around at Mike seeking a sign of acknowledgement for my thoughts. I received none.

Looking forward to freshening up, we entered the hotel. We had no trouble renting a share room at a small cost from Bill the booking clerk. When I picked up the pen to enter our names in the register, his eyes were drawn to the star birthmark on my wrist. I was familiar with this, as I have always had people stare when my sleeve was drawn back, but it rarely caused a comment.

This time however, I suddenly felt self-conscious as if the star was a fascinating oddity. He dragged his gaze away to study the name I was writing in his guest register.

"Greg Allen?"

He scrutinised my face.

"Yes, why?"

"You remind me of someone. You look similar, especially in the face. The surname's the same too, and you have the same mark."

"Must be thinking of someone else. I've never been here before."

Mike butted in. "Don't tell me someone else has the same ugly 'dial' of a face you have?" His ever-ready laughter came to the fore as he spoke.

The staring clerk blinked several times as if to clear his vision. He changed the subject. "You're so welcome. Let me know if you need anything." He spoke directly at me, ignoring Mike. "You'll find your room, No 13, upstairs. The one other Allens have used. It's kept ready for err . . . any further visitors."

"What other Allens?" I was curious.

Bill flopped back into his chair, a puzzled expression on his face. "I can't remember. I'm not sure why I said that, but it'll come to me later. I'll tell you then."

He's got a screw loose. I've never heard of Rockville before today. I don't know of any Allen, in or outside, the immediate family who has what he called 'the mark'. It doesn't matter if he can't remember, but I'll still ask him tomorrow just in case he does. I never did.

I changed the subject. "I'm curious about the town. Give me a run-down."

Mike intervened. "You're not still looking for info for that diary of yours are you? I heard you promise you'd keep one covering the trip, so it could be printed up in the University newspaper."

"Ignore him, Bill. Tell us what this place is like. Is there much activity, especially at night?"

My question went unheeded. Bill commenced to give us a picturesque description of the area. He told us that the town was nestled into a narrow strip of low land on the edge of the sea. It butted up against a low rugged mountain. It had one main street and a population of around thirty permanent dwellers. It was bordered in other directions by cliffs and mountains pitted by mining. "On the top of the mountain, which overlooks a small cove stands . . ." He paused.

I finished the sentence for him. "Vine-strangled ruins staring out over both land and ocean. We noticed them on our way here."

Bill seemed deep in thought for a few moments. He then recommenced speaking. He told us that the cove was at the base of the mountain. The hotel, and the adjoining park beside it, bordered the cove. He claimed that the cove itself was behind rock walls, and only accessible from the top, via steps hewn into the cliff face of the mountain. These solid rock guardians stood fast against both the gentle lapping of the sea and the fierce crashing of the surf. This developed into a roar when sucked into the cove by strong unpredictable currents. The cove with its secluded beach had always been, from ancient times, washed by moody tides. These surged in endlessly between lower piles of green slime-covered rocks, which kept the park itself and hotel grounds protected from the ocean's fury. Rock sculptures stabbed upward, piercing air and mist, to form high walls that travelled seaward, only to sink from sight well out at sea. These made the cove seem impregnable.

Mike interrupted, "Greg!" He was now in one of his impatient moods and jerked his head towards the stairs. He began to walk away. He had already grabbed our large, brass room keys, so I turned and quickly joined him. We hurried in the direction the clerk had indicated.

After showering and changing we made our way to the dining room, where we hungrily ate a generous meal of bacon, sausages, and scrambled eggs. Locally baked bread, toasted, and with lashings of butter, adorned our side dish. No other diners were in the room. It dawned on me that we had not seen anyone except the clerk and the waiter, nor any other vehicles anywhere. I mentioned it to Mike.

"Who cares?" Mike shrugged. "It's early, so they're probably at home. Want to make a bet we'll find a few locals in the bar, even at this hour? "

"No thanks."

The waiter returned. Mike, in his typical way, tried to embarrass me. "He . . ." Mike thumbed in my direction. "wants to know where everybody is, 'specially the good looking chicks?"

"It's always quiet at this time," was the quick reply as he walked away, carrying our discarded plates.

"See Greg, there's a logical reason for everything." Mike smiled, playfully poking my shoulder as he spoke. He continued in the deep voice reminiscent of our Professor of Psychology at Uni. "You shouldn't let that imaginative literary mind of yours find spooks everywhere, young Greg."

Mike was correct. My imagination did have a tendency to get away from me. However, by the time we were ready to indulge in our usual thirst quenchers I had lost all apprehension about the town.

We made our way to the public bar and gave our orders to the man behind the counter. An older man sidled up to us as we waited. It was obvious he wanted to chat to us. He stretched his lips wide in what I assumed was a welcome smile and said, "New in town aren't ya? We'll make ya welcome. Come and join me . . . I'm Jack . . . and me mates. We're sitting at that table near the window."

"Why not?" Mike said. Clutching glasses of beer we followed him to his table where we joined two others. One old bloke, Charlie, took more than normal interest in me. "I know you."

"No, sorry. We've never met."

"You've the same eyes and the same hair."

"Everyone has a double they say, a doppelganger." *Maybe mine's that other visitor the clerk mentioned. It'd be interesting to meet him."* I was about to ask more, but I was interrupted.

"What are you drinking?" enquired the other one. He scoffed when I replied, "beer." The others joined him in insisting, 'no beer, only whiskey'. I was not up to drinking much whiskey, but as they say, ' When in Rome, do as the Romans do.' I would revert back to beer at the next round.

The talk from our new friends turned to local happenings. This merged into strange outbursts from Jack, who, judging from his appearance and actions, seemed mentally unbalanced.

The group went on to tell us, that at this time in every leap year, the wind, rushing, whistling, and shaking the town, slams in from somewhere out at sea. The ocean itself responds with questing waves towering and roaring menacingly. "The people in the township," they added, "stop what they are doing whenever they hear maniacal laughter and what some believe are screams. It impales a cold chill of fear into the residents. It all happens worse around midnight on February 29th, when the winds drive clouds across a full moon."

Charlie nodded. "It'll happen tonight 'cos its February 29th." He leaned back in his chair and picked up his glass.

Jack, well into his drinking, and with eyes bulging, added, "There's a full moon tonight. The clouds are already riding on the lap of the wind. That's when we hear the Voice on the Wind. That's what we here call it. It comes on the wind's wings from up there." He pointed to the cliff top, as one of his companions gave a deep sigh.

Jack's wild statement was enough to trigger off sarcasm from Mike. "Don't tell me." Mike spoke in a mocking tone. "This voice wouldn't come from those ruins on the mountain, would it? A laughing, screaming ghost with its own ruins to haunt . . . great stuff." Mike began to laugh. All signs of a relaxed atmosphere dissipated.

Jack, still staring out the window, spat his words in Mike's direction. "Wait and see, unbeliever. Hear the wind out there now? It's them Evil Ones from the depths of hell comin'." He paused, head cocked to one side as if listening. "Can't you hear 'em laughin'?"

The roar of the sea became extremely loud, even through the closed windows and lined walls of the hotel. I had heard other seas as loud, when king tides and westerly winds came crashing in to belt the shore during bad storms. I listened intently, but could hear nothing resembling laughter or screams in the whistling and thundering.

"Shut up Jack," spoke Paul as he tried to appeal to Jack's common sense. "You're making a damn fool of yourself."

Jack shook his head, determined to continue. "All we want is peace . . . to be at rest."

I asked the obvious question. "Have you thought of getting the police to sort it out? It could be someone's idea of a joke."

"We have in the past. They came, looked around, and went. They claimed they heard and saw nothing. They told us to give up the grog. They said that Jack was suffering the D.Ts from alcoholic poisoning. They even accused us of inventing it all to attract tourists."

"Then why don't you locals go and chase this . .whatever it is . . . away . . . this Voice on the Wind, if it upsets everyone?" asked the still grinning Mike.

"We have to wait, until . . ." Jack looked at me, but hesitated before he continued. "People are too scared. Only strangers ever go up to the top of the mountain. Maybe they go out of curiosity . . . to investigate. They don't come back." After that outburst Jack, apparently exhausted, settled down and this caused the others to relax.

An amusing story we thought, so, after a few more drinks we encouraged them to tell us more. They were reluctant, but drink makes a resistant mind more cooperative. "Come on Jack, tell us more about this Voice on the Wind." I was becoming as patronising as Mike, but unlike Mike I was fascinated by the tale. Jack appeared hesitant, while the others began to shake their heads more ominously. This increased my curiosity.

After downing another drink Jack's tongue began to loosen again. "The wind," Jack whispered in a low mysterious way. We leaned closer to him so we would not miss a word. "If you're fearless enough to go up there, the wind'll tell you a story."

"The wind tells a story?" Mike's eyes danced with scepticism. We both dismissed it as nothing more than a bar yarn, great to tell our mates back at college.

Our new companions reacted nervously to our amusement. There was silence for a few minutes, until Jack draped himself halfway across the table. With limbs loose like those of a rag doll, he reiterated, "If you're brave enough to go up there, the wind will tell you a story . . . true as I'm sittin' 'ere."

"Are you sure it's the wind that tells a story, Jack? Perhaps there's a ghost up there waiting to devour innocent maidens, which we're not? What a great yarn Jack. It's the best bar-room tale we've heard yet."

After a few minutes Jack began to mumble. "Do you know whose voice is the Voice on the Wind? It belongs to . . ."

"Jack, shut ya trap," Paul interrupted, cutting him short. Immediately Charlie intervened. He asked us how we liked the town. It put an end to Jack's comments. He had dampened the gaiety around us. However, his silence came too late for Mike and me. Jack had set in motion a chain of events that would change our lives. But if anyone else had heard Jack's ravings about the Voice on the Wind that day, they would not have blamed us for not taking him seriously.

I patted him on the back. "Good story old man. Have another whiskey . . . my shout." After the next drink Jack's head hit the table. He was out to it.

"Don't worry about Jack. He loves being melodramatic," spoke up Paul as he tapped his temple. "He was almost killed after being whipped by the boss, Lord Flurice Westley. He and Lady Phoebe have the

Manor House on the top of the mountain. He owns everything, the town, the quarries, and us. We're in that lot too."

"I can see Jack's not acting quite normal, but what' he talking about? Does he link his 'Voice on the Wind' with the Westleys and their Manor?" I asked.

"Give it a break." Mike jumped in, and then lowered his voice. "You don't believe what that drunken old fool was raving about, do you Greg?"

Paul ignored Mike. He stared with narrowed eyes deep into mine to make certain he had my full attention. *Why single me out?* "Son, truth and untruths have many faces in life. It's up to each of us to decide which one to accept. Jack's chosen his."

Mike knew I had become very curious, and he knew I hated to leave a mystery unexplained. "I'll bet you fifty dollars and half a dozen beers, that you're not game to go to the top of the mountain and talk to this 'Voice on the Wind.'" He was trying to milk it for all it was worth.

"Up there? No way!"

"Go up to the top, and be back at midday. See if you can hear the Voice and see any ghosts roaming around moaning, or rattling their chains." He again laughed.

"Not on your life!" I insisted, while slowly shaking my head to make my point, although to take fifty dollars from tight-fisted Mike was a huge temptation. The beer would be a bonus. "If you're so interested, you go, or come with me," I suggested.

"Not me . . . you're the one who's curious. I can see it in your face. Your writer's brain is always sucked in by a good story. Just think what a beaut yarn it will make to add to that diary you're keeping."

"Come on Mike, I'm not that gullible."

"You're scared. That's the problem, admit it."

"I'm not, and you know it."

"Then prove it. Accept the bet. If you don't, you're a wimp," he taunted. "I'll tell our mates back home that 'Mr. Tough Guy', the captain of our footy team, was scared of a talking wind, gale, or whatever." Alcohol was clouding Mike's senses. He would not let up. It must have affected me also. After I had reverted back to drinking only beer, I reconsidered.

"Make it a hundred of those dollars you won, and you're on." I was not immune to accepting a dare if the stakes were high enough. Mike eagerly agreed. I knew he thought I would back down, due to the inertia of my limbs after straddling the bike for so long that day.

The three locals tried to talk all at once, and in unison shook their heads. Paul spoke their ill-concealed thoughts. "You're very foolish. You heard Jack. The others never returned. We never saw them again."

A bet's a bet, and I'll be richer by a hundred dollars. It'll be like taking candy from a baby. I was now obsessed with getting one over Mike. I knew he would embarrass me in front of our friends for the next twelve months if I did not accept, but that did not worry me too much. In winning I would have the pleasure of watching Mike wheeling and dealing, trying his best to get out of handing over the money. Mike only showed eagerness to part with money when involved in some form of gambling. He would bet on two flies crawling up a window, or what some of our mates would say, 'Mike would try to avoid shouting if a shark bit him.'

"I'll drink to your success old mate." Mike spoke sarcastically. A noisy jubilant Mike then gave me the thumbs-up. The silence of the others was tangible. This strange mood of the old men unsettled me.

We left the hotel to walk outside. The main street was deserted. Mike once again began egging me on, saying he was seeing me off on my epic journey into the unknown. With his usual grin he pointed at the cliffs ahead, with their darker, sinister crown. "I'll see you later Greg. My drinking partners and I will wait for your triumphant return. Don't forget to say 'g'day' to the wind for me, but only after it's said 'g'day' to you of course." His laughter made me more determined. *The boot'll be on the other foot' when I get back.*

"I'll go and get my coat. There could be an arctic wind blowing up there." I had no intention of neglecting my creature comfort.

Mike said, "A wind with a chilling story to tell."

"You're hilarious, you know that," I threw back at him as I left him standing there.

I returned to our room. There, I fitted myself with some 'essentials'. I stuffed my torch into my pocket. I did not think I would need it, but decided I might if I wanted to avoid tripping, should there be rubbish inside the ruins. I put two cans of beer, a pub sandwich and some fruit I had taken from the counter, into my backpack. I dropped my camera into my pocket. I would be ready to prove I'd been there, should Mike doubt I had actually been to the ruins themselves. I was now ready to tackle the uphill climb.

Mike was waiting outside with a few new faces I had not seen before. He was no longer smiling, although he managed a sheepish expression. "I'm calling the bet off Greg. I was only joking. Come back inside." He tried to take my arm, but I pulled away.

"Only if you pay up."

"Forget it Greg."

"Then I'll see you later."

As I brushed past him, Mike jumped in front of me, planting two hands on my chest, pushing me back. "Come on man," he pleaded, serious for the first time that day. "It was a joke. Don't leave me alone in this dump of a backwater, drinking with a bunch of ancient guys. Just look at the place. The only excitement is a talking wind. It's stagnating waters here mate. There's no television sets. There's nothing. Even their phones don't work. It's to do with the lord's decree or something. It beats me."

He seemed to think I was angry with him. I was irritable perhaps, but parting with a hundred dollars would teach him a lesson. It would cause him to think carefully about making bets with anyone he could entice into accepting a wager. Mike tried to pull me by the arm back into the hotel. I pulled away. My irritability was quickly turning into annoyance. "To you everything's always one big joke. The bet's on, and you're paying up as soon as I get back."

I walked off, leaving him with the curious locals. One shouted, 'You're a fool, but good luck. Ya'll need it if that evil lord gets ya." I ignored the implications.

"See you at around midday. Keep the beer cold," I called back over my shoulder, as I walked briskly away from them.

CHAPTER 8

Greg hears a Voice. Is the 'Voice on the Wind' real?

At first their voices were loud and clear, but began to die out as the men disappeared back inside the hotel.

I knew some private betting would be organised by Mike. It would be on how long I would stay on the mountain before being petrified by cold, boredom, or both, and hurried back to the hotel.

The feeling of bravado I felt earlier was quickly evaporating as the comforting lights and sounds of the pub softened and melted into thin air. The only company I had as I trudged onward were sentinel-like streetlight posts standing as if at attention along the side of the road. The wind had dropped considerably. The only other sound, apart from the waves caressing the shoreline, was an occasional burst of laughter, or a happy shout, filtering from the hotel.

I knew that ahead of me was a climb up a road with a steep grade in parts, judging from the height of the cliff, to a ruin I was not interested in. I hoped that I would not curse myself for being stupid in not heeding the warnings I had been given. But, I had committed myself, so I would see it through. When I returned I would use the photos I take to show anyone who voiced any doubt about whether or not I did reach the wrecked house.

Perhaps I'm a bigger fool than Mike, taking him on, but it'll teach him a much-needed lesson not to make silly bets. It'll also prove to the locals there's nothing but folklore behind their Voice on the Wind. I had heard winds whining and whistling before; in such a way one could imagine they were trying to form words. I was convinced that here in Rockville it would prove to be a similar scene.

I recalled the blokes at the hotel telling us that to reach the top one had to first find the steps. In Jack's ravings he mentioned stone steps that were not far past the park that lay between the hotel and the base of the cliff. These then changed into a winding track to the top. Paul had said that the only other way up was over a large brick wall, then into the cove and up stairs dug into the cliff itself, which did not warrant even the slightest interest. I was not looking forward to making the climb, but the other alternative, of losing the bet, was not worth considering. Once up there I would find a spot out of the wind where I could to stretch out and relax. Perhaps I could even get some sleep.

The wind dropped, and a heavy stillness followed. *The quiet before the storm?* It seemed to hang over me, leaving me in an unexplainable nervousness.

Walking through overgrown vegetation growing at the base of the cliff, I was thankful that my alcohol intake had not lessened my instinct for self-preservation. I swept aside the tangle of bushes in an attempt to locate the steps.

A gap I found in the bushes exposed the cream coloured surface of a sandstone slab. It did not fit the description Jack had given, but it was a step. I took a photo to show the old man that his description of the steps was wrong. Probing with both feet and hands I found the next steps appeared to be hewn out of the hard earth, as were the rest. *Maybe it's the wrong way, but does it matter? It's still uphill.*

I began my upward trek as a half-blind man, forced to thrust aside wild offshoots that in places almost obscured the pathway. Even the ridged soles of my boots could not prevent my feet slipping at times on loose gravel or topsoil.

Unwilling to dwell on my discomfort, I switched my thoughts to more important matters, such as whether I had brought enough beer with me. It was thirsty work.

On reaching the crest I found myself facing rusted gates teetering on broken hinges – their pattern and design in tangled evidence of a once grand entrance. *To what?* I pressed one of the supporting posts. It fell with a resounding hollow protest. Something flapped overhead. Was it a seagull? As I could not see any sign of life from anything else, I felt I had imagined it. I moved along a path that wound itself through the remains of garden beds, still separated by brick edging. Some were intact though black with mould, and slimy with moss. The spectral remains of broken statues lay half hidden under a blanket of weeds.

I was forced to bend low to pass under overhanging tree branches that formed an archway above me. My boots crunched on beds of dry leaves. The further I walked the louder the crackling of leaves sounded beneath my feet. Engrossed in what was happening underfoot I almost hit my head against a low rotting beam. It was slung across one of the openings into the mass of jumbled timber directly in front of me. The ruins themselves were massive. Judging from the charred pillars lying amidst the piles of debris, it was obvious that it had once been a large building. It was now a mess of broken and decaying timber. Sections of walls had remained standing. They had once supported part of a roof, or, perhaps the floor to an upper level. As the building had collapsed, openings were created amongst the debris. They gave me the impression of a row of gaping hungry mouths. Clinging, rampant vines also subjugated them. They looked ready to swallow all who ventured into their depths. I pulled out my camera and photographed all that was around me. With my light I probed the inside of the nearest dark section. If I wanted to get out of the moody wind I would have to venture within.

Scrambling over mounds of crumbling wood and into a cave-like section, I found what seemed to be a secure wall still standing. It had a supporting post that appeared to be more solid than some of the others. On one side was a pile of bricks suggesting it was once an open fireplace with a brick chimney. With the post, it was helping to support a portion of the wall and a section of roof above it. That was enough to provide some overhead protection. The post itself stood sentinel-like over a patch of uncluttered dirt. There was enough room, when seated, for me to spread myself out. I leaned my weight against the wall to test it. It did not move. I pushed against the post, to shake it from its foundations if possible, but it refused to move even slightly. I concluded it was sufficiently sturdy, and would not fall should any squall descend on the place. Something gritty had coated my hands in the process. It was black soot. Obviously a fire had been through the original building – a lightning strike perhaps?

As it could be risky to continue any further through the gaping openings adjoining my chosen spot, I settled myself down on the ground. With my back against the post I made myself as comfortable as I could, to wait out the time. I opened a can of beer and sipped it. I hoped to doze off, although I could feel an element of excitement, which made me smile with satisfaction. I pictured Mike's one hundred dollars clutched in my fist. This would be so easy.

I began to relax. The clouds had, for the moment at least, been scattered by the wind. I looked out at the expanse of space visible through the missing overhead section, and fanciful thoughts tumbled over one another. The pale blue of the sky had formed a distant backdrop to fluffy clouds. I wished I had brought a pen and pad to write my thoughts down as a basis for a poem I could write.

No wind was gushing through this part of the ruins when I entered. The atmosphere had been as heavy as a shroud. Now, with cruel suddenness, a blast of cold air whipped around the protective wall catching me unawares. I shivered as the wind groaned, screeched, and whistled, doubling its strong reverberation. At its urging, long whip-thin tendrils of a sucking creeper, like those of a starving octopus, sought me out. They created swishing, hollow, tapping sounds as they swung and clawed towards me. It was as if the plant, using its feelers to seek out food, was attempting to wrap them around me, perhaps to hug me to death? *My mind's playing tricks. Get over it.*

I longed for the unawareness of sleep. If not, I knew there would be some lonely, and uncomfortable, hours ahead. When the wind had again scuttled off somewhere I tried to will myself to nod off. Slowly the 'window shades' of my eyes drooped and closed. I shut out all thought as I listened to the sound of distant music created by the rolling waves caressing the stretch of shore below. I drifted like a lily on a stream towards the waiting arms of sleep.

As I travelled down this corridor within my mind, the banging of loose timber somewhere behind me kept in rhythm with the waves turning on themselves and on each other. It did not disturb me unduly. Falling further from the known present, my mind, without effort, conjured up images of others. They were men, who by their appearance, could have passed for close relatives. They seemed to be trying to tell me something but I could not hear what it was. They drifted into my semi-conscious world, only to disappear again.

The next thing I became aware of, was someone mumbling in the doorway of my mind. I jerked my chin up in surprise as the wind, reborn, intensified. *What new dream is this, or is it only the wind groaning through the ruins?* Several whispered sentences separated themselves from the whistling and swishing. The voice was thin. It sounded like a child's. I waited for it to continue. I wanted to be certain I actually heard a voice. If more words followed, they had dissipated before reaching my ears. *What am I thinking? I'm getting as bad as the locals, hearing voices.* My mind sought an explanation. *Perhaps Mike's sneaked up after me, and is playing tricks on me. Yes that's it!*

Having been startled awake, I shouted, "Okay Mike. I know it's you. You've had your fun, now show yourself." I waited, but only silence met my outburst. Mike could be so exasperating at times, but enough was enough. I scrambled to my feet. I stumbled and collided with wreckage in a futile attempt to search at least this section of the ruins for a jubilant Mike. I shone my limited light as far as it would reach inside several of the darkened enclosures.

I walked to where I could look down the cliff to the sea. Seeing no one I moved to the edge of the path I had climbed to get to the top. There too I saw nothing, except for some dancing shadows waltzing across the land, caused by the wind and the rays of the sun combined.

On returning to my chosen spot I heard that whisper again. Was the voice real or imagined? I was uncertain. I knew it was not Mike's. He could not have changed his deep voice to such a high pitch. *Perhaps he's brought someone with him.* Mike was capable of carrying out such a hoax. All I needed to do was wait. When Mike made his next move I was determined to catch him out.

A renewed burst of wind displayed no mercy as it struck me. It screamed with such velocity it left me with an all-consuming feeling of anxiety. Its coldness stole all the warmth from my body. I felt as if I could be sucked out, picked up like a dry leaf, and blown out to sea, to be lost forever. *Perhaps the ones who never came back became fish food.*

This precocious wind had unnerved me. I looked about for something to secure myself to the spot. Still upright, I clung to the pitted post – my body rigid. Every muscle became locked against the anticipation of being dragged away into the void. Then, as quickly as the wind descended upon me, threatening and menacing, it dropped away, drawing its power within itself, leaving me in a vacuum of creeping panic.

Where's the 'voice' during all that? Was its owner snatched up and dumped elsewhere? I believed I had company, but how could I be certain? What I did know was that deserted places attracted undesirables. Some could be running from the law – a grave concern in my present predicament

I leaned over, still with one hand spread wide against the post for support. I felt around with the other for something I had seen earlier. It was a reasonably solid length of wood. I almost lost my balance in the process of picking it up, but managed to keep upright by pressing myself back against the post. I wanted to be prepared for whatever, or whoever, might come close. Isolated in the semi-darkness of this semi- enclosed section, the lone piece of wood now in my moist grip became a comfort. I held my breath, ready for the unknown. My eyes still kept probing one dull patch, then another, scanning each gaping hole, but seeing nothing; nor were any footprints in evidence in the visible area.

A soft breeze that stroked my face with the gentleness of a baby's hand now replaced the easing wind. It reminded me of my little sister Aimie. I was grateful, as it broke the spell of trepidation I was under. The voice came again, breaking the heavy burden of suspense that impaled me. It seemed to be a youngster's voice. *Am I losing it? Going whacko . . . defending myself against a kid? If it is a kid and not some weirdo.*

I slid to the ground, partly with relief. Seated now, I groped around until I found a can of beer. It had rolled away when I threw down my bag. I flicked it open, gulped it down and burped – a slice of normality in the midst of what was becoming an absurd scenario. It did not last.

"Hello. I'm Joseph," said a childish voice. The voice was now low and soft, almost sing-songy. I could no longer dismiss it as imagination. "Please sir, I want to tell you a story. Please listen, please," begged the voice.

A kid for sure, but this is too absurd for words . . . a story? What, here and now? He's weird. Realising the immature voice could only belong to a young boy, my nervous tension began to slowly disperse. I loosened my grip on the piece of wood, but still held it in readiness should anything more unexpected eventuate.

He must have been unsure as to whether I heard him, for his voice became louder.

"Mr Allen . . . Greg . . . please listen," he pleaded.

How does he know my name? He's probably a Little Big Ears sneaking around town all day listening to adults talking. I thought I could hear breathing, but could see nothing. I realised he had the protection of darkness, wherever he was hiding, whereas I was obviously visible to him. Even when the sun escaped the clouds, it failed to light up all the dim corners and crevice-filled inky blackness in this jungle of a ruined building.

He cried louder, in obvious desperation to be heard. "Please, I don't want you to die." *Die? Who else is hiding up here? That old man, Jack, said some never came back. Were they murdered? Is this child warning me to leave before I get killed? Ridiculous!* But, I was almost completely defenceless. The fear of an unexpected and possible fatal attack took root. *Is it all a sick joke? It must be. What kid would be up here alone? Mike has gone too far this time, or is it some maniac from the village roaming loose?* I told myself that my imagination was galloping away again, when an idea surfaced. "Well, if you want to play games, come out from wherever you're hiding so I can see you." I challenged him in the belief he would, if genuine, do as I requested.

"I . . . I can't . . . not yet," came the response.

"Why? You're alone aren't you?"

"Yes, yes, Greg Allen, I am. I come early. So did them others, 'cause you're early. I want to tell you about the evil ones. You're in real bad danger." *Old Jack's song again.*

"You're family," said the voice. *Sure . . . we're all part of the world's human family. The boy's psycho, but hardly dangerous.* I felt the fear of immediate danger was unfounded. If someone wanted to attack me they could have done so already. I breathed more easily. I did not ask him to explain the absurdity of what he was saying. I assumed it must be Mike's doing; concocting this little pantomime to force me back at the hotel before midday and lose the bet. *Let Mike carry on. I'll wait for him to slip up. He'll end up not being able to stop himself laughing, and give the game away. I know him.*

I adopted an indifferent tone, hoping to get the message across that I was not really interested. "I'm too pooped to argue with you. Tell your story, whatever it is, if you have one, then go home and leave me in peace." I did not need one of Mike's crazy little games. I intended to collect one hundred dollars from him regardless. I would sit it out and see what eventuated. I squirmed into a more comfortable position on the lumpy earth.

A childish excited voice again arrowed towards me. "Thank you, thank you, Greg."

My bored tone had obviously gone over his head, or perhaps this was a recording, with Mike and his mates hidden out of sight. That would account for the boy not coming close enough for me to see him. I closed my eyes and waited for him to begin. It would fill in time, and with luck I would doze off for a while. There was no response. *Why's he stopped talking? Is he creeping closer?* I gripped the piece of wood lying across my knees tighter. I raised it higher, hoping I would not have to use it.

"What's on your mind that's so important? Come on. Get on with it. I could do with a good story to pass the time," I called to him.

I heard what sounded like childish sobs. It reminded me of my little sister when she cried. Whether it was a hoax or he was crazy, something was upsetting him. Against my will I was feeling a change in my attitude. I was becoming convinced the sorrow was genuine. U*nless it's Mike's way to get me to weaken. Oh yes, I'll make a guess. The kid's going to want me to take him back to his distraught parents, before noon of course.*

"I want your help" *Here it comes.* "To stop the evil ones from killing any more."

"What? You've raving." *And I thought I had a good imagination.*

"Please, if you won't leave now, please listen." His tone had reverted to pleading. It affected me to the point that I was seesawing between belief in his genuineness, and disbelief in a real child's existence. *If Mike's behind this he needs to improve his lines . . . evil ones? Do better than that Mike. They're Jack's lines.*

"If you have a problem with these evil ones, why ask a visitor for help? There's a bunch of locals down there." Waiting for an answer I decided I would go along with whatever Mike, or Jack and his friends, were laying on me. Creepy or not, I would stick it out. I could not wait to feel Mike's crisp one hundred dollar note in my hand. I deserved it, after all the rubbish he was loading on me. He would not scare me into leaving early. Meanwhile, the voice would make the time go faster.

"I'm only a stranger passing through," I said, and added. "What about your mum and dad?" I wondered why his parents were not out looking for him if he were genuine.

He evaded my question for a few moments then spoke slowly. "I live with Aunt Mavis. She's like my mum. I never know my other mum."

"What's your name?"

"Joseph Allen."

"I don't believe you." *He must be some actor well versed in his craft. Trust Mike to find another Allen, if he is an Allen. The name's common enough. The hotel clerk and others seemed to think they'd seen me before. Maybe distant relatives live somewhere around here.*

I now grew more interested in what he would say next. I relaxed. I felt that by talking, I could lead him back to why he said I was in danger. Meanwhile, I would have to be patient. *I'll keep playing along until I get an opening. I'll keep up my side of the conversation.*

"I'm an Allen too as you obviously know. I'm a student. I study literature at the Queensburg University. What about you?" I was trying to change the subject, to catch him out, and perhaps distract him from the distress he seemed to be suffering. He replied without hesitation. I was on the right track.

"I never been to school. I look after Aunt Mavis' garden. I like the garden, but my beach's the best. It's in the cove. I know a secret way to get through the rocks and over the wall. No one knows, just me." His voice dropped." Lord Westley, and them, has to use the steps they dug in the cliff." A sound like a short laugh followed.

"Is this the Lord Westley who owns everyone and everything?"

"Yes . . . you won't tell him?"

"Your secret's safe with me." I replied with a sigh, hoping Mike or whoever was behind this, would give up soon. Mike would know nothing about any local beach, so I tried to trick him. "Tell me about your beach."

"It's closed in, sort of, 'cept the sea part. The water's real deep. I found a sandbank. I can swim. Uncle Pete taught me. I can dive too, and there's a cave where I take my clothes off 'cos nobody can see." Joseph laughed, apparently with pleasure as he bathed in the mental imagery of 'his' beach. He became silent. I thought he may have finished and I could revert to the question of my own personal danger, but he started off again. "I was the only one to go there 'till Lord Westley and his Lady came. The beach was mine! All mine! It belonged to me. They stole it off me." *Now it's getting interesting.*

Joseph kept talking, expounding details of his beach. It was difficult for me not to doze off, but, between those short naps I forced myself to listen, as I would listen to little Aimie's stories involving her 'doll of the moment'.

Assuming he was telling the truth, it meant that, to him, it was a hide-away that he believed only he knew about. That must have ended when Lord Westley arrived after his uncle died, and took over the Manor House that the old fellows talked about. *Westley seems to have upset everyone around here, especially this boy.*

Joseph became quiet again. In the nothingness, despite my doubts, I still wanted to know how the story/hoax would end. A strange bond of empathy was developing between this unseen boy and myself. *If by chance there is a real child out there I'll show some interest.*

"Are you sure you don't go to school?" I was anxious to compare this voice with eleven-year-old Aimie's, to more correctly decide his age.

"Aunt Mavis teach me. She says I'm lucky 'cause I never growed up . . . like Peter Pan. He never went to school . . . like me."

"How old are you Joseph?"

"Fifteen."

"I thought you were . . ."

"Do you think I talk not good for fifteen, or I'm stu . . . pid?"

"Don't put words into my mouth," I said bluntly. "What I was going to say is that you sound younger than fifteen." The truth was becoming clearer. Like using pieces in a jigsaw puzzle, a picture was forming in my mind. It could explain why his voice had not yet broken. He was a boy who would never grow to full maturity as other boys would. I guessed that was why his aunt protected him from going to normal school. Perhaps it was the reason his parents, if they were still alive, or had more children to care for, had sent him to his aunt for her to raise. His attachment to his beach sprouted from a desire to belong. He would not have had much in common with other boys his age.

I knew I was being sucked in as I began to feel concerned in a vague, protective sort of way, but I decided, for his sake, I would escort him back to his aunt's place, wherever that was. I could leave him at her door, hide out until midday, and then return to the hotel. *That's cheating, but it'll serve Mike right.*

"Joseph! I think it's wise if I walk you home. Your aunt must be worried sick about you, wandering up here all on your own. It could be dangerous." *Now I'll see him face to face and find out the truth.*

"NO! . . . No . . . no." His feverish cries held frustration more than anger. "I haven't told you my story yet. I haven't got to the real bad part."

Out of nowhere the cold wind bonded with his words and attacked as if emulating his distress, hurling leaves and debris towards me with the same fury as it had several times before. I huddled against the wall, attempting to protect my body warmth from being stolen again, by the wind. *What a place! Who in their right mind would live here?* I called out as loudly as I was capable of. "Are you all right out there? Answer me, damn it."

He spoke again. "Yes sir." The wind stopped as suddenly as it had begun.

I was quickly on my feet in readiness. I began to collect my pack. I would bring this nonsense to a head.

"Joseph, I've told you. I'm taking you home now!" I expected him to walk out into the open and be visible at last.

"No! You promise you'd listen to my story."

"Don't argue. Let's go."

"You promised. You did." There was a catch in his voice.

I weakened. "Okay then." I concurred, purely because I knew the situation was hopeless until he finished what he wanted to say. Also, at the back of my mind was the knowledge that I still had a few hours to fill in before I could rightly collect my winnings. I returned to my previous position, wishing I were somewhere more comfortable, in fact, anywhere else but in these ghostly ruins with company I could not see, only hear.

Joseph had become, for me, the Voice on the Wind.

CHAPTER 9

Greg is held captive by the Voice.

In the now brooding silence, broken only by the murmur of the sea, I tried to ease my head into a more comfortable position. My neck was stiff. *I must have dozed off.* For a moment I wondered where I was. Slowly, in my half-awake state, I became aware that, for the second time since this bizarre encounter began, the sun was no longer shielded behind dark menacing clouds. It was poised as if stationary in the area of sky that was visible to me. The sun and the sky have always been of little interest to me. Neither have I embraced the moon, even as a romantic symbol. Today I craved for the sun's rays to keep breaking through what was a seemingly impenetrable cloud-cover, to spread warmth, and light up the dark caverns in this grim place. My feeling of isolation in this dome of limited vision grew. I began to feel I was the last human left on earth. In this poised stillness I discounted Joseph. *If not Mike's creation, he must be a dream or figment of my imagination. I probably conjured him up by weaving an imagined person to keep me company, born out of the eeriness of the place.*

    The boy's voice, rising sharply in response to my inattention, interrupted and discounted this flight into fantasy. He seemed determined to take up his ridiculous story again. "Lord Westley and Lady Phoebe are bad people. Aunt Mavis says they're rich 'cos they own everything. Everyone hates them and their big Manor House. Aunt Mavis says it's not the Aussie way to lord it over everyone. I hated them 'cos they took my beach, like it was theirs. He beat me too." I could almost feel him shudder in the pause that followed this outburst. "They like lots of parties. They talk and laugh real loud. Aunt Mavis says it's 'cos they're always drunk. They stopped me going on my beach. They chased me away. I wanted them to go somewhere else, so I could have my beach back."

"Where's this Manor House you keep mentioning?" I had not noticed any building when I reached the top. As it was impossible to see very far beyond the range of thick vegetation and closely standing trees, I assumed there could be more buildings of some kind on this level section of the mountain.

"You'll see it tonight, when Lord Westley comes. Everything else is early 'cos you come early. He don't want you to leave," was the strange reply. *That's too bad. I won't be here. I'm going to be far away from this place before then.*

"I never told Aunt Mavis 'bout my beach 'cos she said don't go there. It was risky she said, 'cos the Westleys'd get mad, but I did. I watched when they put up them little huts they change their clothes in. Aunt Mavis calls them blemishes, you know, like pimples." He paused. "One night I sneaked out to the beach real late. I pushed the sheds over. They looked so funny, wobbling like Lord Westley when he drinks too much brandy and other stuff. I wanted to cry when he put them back up. I didn't know what to do. I try hard to think." With a catch in his voice Joseph stopped talking.

"Why didn't you tell somebody how you felt?"

"I couldn't tell Aunt Mavis or Pete. Pete's our best friend. He comes from some place a long way away. He sticks up for me, like when some kids whisper like I can't hear them. They say. 'He's . . . you know.' and tap the side of their heads when they say it. When Pete shouts at them, they run away. I don't care 'bout them. I got the birds to talk to and I had to think. The more I think, the more I get mad at Lord Westley.

Lots of times I'm up the mountain to look at what they was doing. Then I hide behind the bushes near the top. I watch the people on the beach. Their music is like saucepans banging together. They make so much noise they shout when they talk. They never find my sandbank further up, or my cave. They ain't very smart. I'm smart, 'cos it was me what found them." After a pause he asked. "They're still mine, ain't they?"

"What Joseph?"

"My beach, and my cave?"

"Of course they are," I agreed in a half-hearted attempt to pacify him. I began reflecting on his hurt feelings, as I would have done if my little sister had been upset. I had to keep reminding myself I would be out of Rockville within a few hours. For now I allowed my imagination to gallop away, especially as Mike was not beside me to make me rein it in. *Perhaps he is, and it's his intention to bore me or frighten me enough to high tail it back to the hotel and lose the bet.*

Joseph was still talking. "One time when I was hiding, someone grabbed the back of my shirt. I tried to run away. My shirt tore. 'Caught ya.' It was Lord Westley what said that. I tried to get away, but I couldn't. He started to say things I didn't know about, like, 'you're nothing but a dirty pervert. You're always perving on us. You need your eyes cut out. Don't think I don't know what you're up to.' Pete said a pervert was a very bad person. Then Lord Westley squeezed my face with them long fingers and sharp pointy nails. It hurt. When he let me go, he hits me so hard he made me cry. I tried to tell him I ain't done nothin' wrong. Then I say 'sorry', but he hits me again. He was grinnin' all the time.

His friend came. He told him to stop. He said I was only a kid and backward to boot, and wouldn't know Arthur from Martha. Lord Westley let me go. I started to run. He shouted after me that if I ever came back he'd rip out my eyes, and do other bad things with a knife as well.

I still cried, 'cos I knew Aunt Mavis would be angry. My shirt was all torn and my pants was wet."

"What did your aunt say when you got home?"

"She don't know."

"Why not?" I demanded, exposing my ever-increasing feelings of pity and concern.

"I was scared. I didn't do nothin' bad did I?"

"No, of course not, but go on." *I have to find out how this turns out.*

"I saw Pete comin'. I tried to hide behind a post, but he saw me. He shouted that he knew it must be Lord Westley what did it. He seen me going up the mountain. I had the sniffles, so I nod. Pete called Lord Westley some bad names that I knew and some I don't. He said that someone ought to put dynamite under Westley and blow him up. That'd get rid of him and his crowd for good.

He took me to his place and cleaned me up. He said he wouldn't tell Aunt Mavis if I promise not to go up the mountain again. He said if I agreed he'd take me to the quarry where he works to see something real good. Pete's a big man at the quarries. I promise, 'cos I always want to see what was there. Aunt Mavis'd never let me. She said only trouble'd come of it."

I frowned, mystified as to why this boy who now held me in a web of his words refused to reveal himself. Joseph and I were now unquestionably roped together in space and words, like early cave seekers in some newly discovered lonely place.

    "Pete said he'd pick me up early in the morning and take me to the quarry when he went to work, though no kids or people who don't work there are 'lowed, 'cos it's real dangerous. He said I'd be okay with him. I got up at sunrise 'cos I couldn't sleep. When he came I asked if I could ride in the back of his truck. 'Okay son', he said. He calls me 'son'.

    At the quarry, men was running everywhere, yelling, tellin' each other what to do. I tried to look everywhere at once. Pete helped me down off the truck. He told me they was going to blast No.1 cliff face. He took hold of my arm and I had to hurry to keep up with him. When a man called out that it mightn't be safe there in a minute, and to take cover, we got down behind a big truck. I put the earmuffs the man threw at us, over my ears, like Pete was doing.

    Men was workin' on what Pete called, I think, blastin' caps and det-natin' cords. I didn't know what he meant but I watched close. I held on to Pete's arm when I saw one of the men go to set them off. Pete shoved me in front of him, close. The cliff made a big noise. The ground shook. It made the truck jump, and me too. Then it all fell down. There was lots of dust. Pete laughed and said I looked like a ghost. He pointed to a real big building. He told me he would have to tell them he was leaving to take me home."

    "Hold on Joseph." I had to interrupt. "I didn't think the quarries existed any more. I haven't seen any activity over in that direction. It looks deserted. In fact I've seen no vehicles at all anywhere."

"They're here, but . . ." He said no more.

I'll check on this when I get back to the hotel. "Are you sure you're not making all this up?"

"I don't tell lies. Aunt Mavis would beat me."

He's probably right. I've only been in the town for a few hours and most of those were spent inside the hotel.

"Pete took me to a big shed. At the door I grabbed on to Pete 'cause I was scared, but Pete said it was okay. Inside was two men. I tried to hide behind Pete 'cos one was Lord Westley. He looked straight at me and smiled horrible. 'We meet again kid,' he said real soft. I wanted to run away but Pete held my arm and told him real nice, 'Leave the kid alone. But Lord Westley kept watching me with his black eyes. He was pulling his lips wide at me and I could see his long dogteeth.

Pete pushed me down on to a chair. He told me to stay put. I couldn't stop starin' at Lord Westley. If he came close I was going to run outside real quick.

There was papers on the table and Pete and another man started to look at them. Lord Westley starts talkin'. I heard him say 'cove', so I listen. He said that the papers he had on the table were to do with the cove. He said he was going to send in men to blow up the rock wall in the park the next day, so he could get in trucks. He said they would push the rocks flat, and then put on lots of the sand, so he could build a small house for his friends. He said he wanted it done for Lady Phoebe's birthday.

I cried out loud. The cove'd be all broken up. There'd be lots more people on my beach. They would find my cave. I ran up to Lord Westley and thumped him on his chest with my fists. I told him he couldn't 'cos it was mine. He slapped me across the face and pushed me away.

Pete got angry and told Lord Westley real loud this time, to leave me alone.

Lord Westley said he shouldn't be bringing a kid to the quarry in the first place.

Pete took me outside. He said to find something to do, but to keep out a trouble as we was leavin' soon. He went back inside. I wiped my face with the back of my hand. Aunt Mavis said I was too big to cry.

I walked round looking at what the men was doing. Then I got sick of doin' nothin', so I climbed on the back of the big big truck. There were lots of boxes, some was open. They was full of the explosive stuff, like what the man used to make the rocks fall down. I 'membered Pete said somebody should blow Lord Westley up. I thought that if I blow up their huts the Westleys'd be angry and go away. Nobody was lookin' so I took some that I hid down me shirt. I did not sleep that night, I thought of what Lord Westley was going to do. I sneaked back real real early the next day, to watch them do it again. When they wasn't' lookin' I took some more."

Surely this is just a yarn. The kid couldn't be thinking of blowing up someone else's property, or could he? My brain burst into active concern. "Joseph, tell me that you made all that up."

"I didn't. It's true."

"You haven't got any of that stuff with you, here now, have you?" There was no answer. *Just part of his idiotic story, but what if is isn't? Can I take the risk?* "Well if you have, I want them, now." I stretched my hand out into empty air, hoping that he would come forward and give it to me, if he really had any. Nothing happened. Fear and uncertainty were, at the same time, electrifying me. They supported a terrible thought of a possible non-existing tomorrow for me as I seemed to be caught up in the plans Joseph was making, or had already made.

From Joseph's lips came a strange, blunt reply, "No, I can't."

"You're off the planet Joseph. If you have any dynamite, do you realise how dangerous it is?" I had to accept the possibility that he was telling the truth.

Joseph snapped back. "I hate him . . . hate him . . . hate him!"

"Stop! Don't you realise what you've done? That's stealing." If it were true, the boy obviously had no idea what the consequences could be. I waited for him to reconsider. At the same time I realised that he saw his world as being destroyed by Lord Westley. It was Wesley's Manor House, Joseph claimed, I would be able to see later. *Will it by then have become another pile of ruins?* I could not dwell upon that. All I knew was that dynamite and deep hatred were not good bedfellows, especially in the hands of a hurt and angry child. "Joseph are you still there?"

"Yes."

Relief swept over me. "Does anyone else know about this plan of yours?" I spoke softly so as not to reveal my own anxiety.

"Only Parson Anderson."

"And what did he tell you?"

"He wasn't happy with me."

"That's fine, just fine. But what have you done with the dynamite? That's if you have any. You don't intend to use it do you?" I fought desperately with my vocal cords to sound casual, as a surge of frustration threatened to make me shout.

"I said. I took it to blow up the huts . . . voom . . . like they done at the quarry, so it'd be my beach again.

When Pete took me home I wanted to go to the cove straight away with the explosives, 'cos I thought Aunt Mavis might find them, but I got scared. If they seen me, they'd beat me bad and take them off me. It's best when it's dark, 'cos no one can see you. I sneak out at night sometimes, when there's a full moon. I like to watch the night birds look for food. They call to each other to come quick when they find some. All the time I kept thinking that tomorrow the beach'll be mine again. When Aunt Mavis was having a rest I didn't want to wait so I take the dynamite and left."

"When did this happen? You're not planning anything like that later today are you, after the Westleys arrive?"

Joseph did not reply. He continued with his story. "I ran along the main street. Once someone came out of a doorway. I ducked behind a post 'til they'd gone.
I got up on to the top of the rocks and saw Lord and Lady Westley down on the beach. They saw me. Lord Westley shouted at me. 'Perv! I'll rip your eyes out if I get hold of you. I'm the Lord of the Manor, so watch out.'

His lady screamed too. 'And I'll carve out your innards. If I died tomorrow I'd come back, just to do that.' Both of them started laughing. They were still laughing when they was going up the steps to their house.

I sat on a rock waiting for them to get to the top. I watched the white foam rolling over and over on the top of the waves, but they was taking so long, I couldn't wait. I climbed along the rocks 'til I got close to the cave, but I had to cross the sand to get to the huts. The Westleys were watching me from the top so I got a good idea. I would come back when it was dark, and put the dynamite behind some rocks, like they did at the quarry. I'd take the cap thing as far away as they'd go and set it off."

Now he's really off with the fairies. This is getting interesting Mike. If it's your doing, I couldn't have thought up anything better myself.

"Tomorrow the beach'll be mine."

Now I've got the picture. The Westleys are arriving later today. Their manor is around here somewhere. Despite Joseph with his warped mind making up this story, perhaps he intends to carry out his threat as he sort of described it. On the other side of the coin, there may have been an explosion here once, hence these ruins, and Joseph is repeating folklore embellished with his own imagination. As for the rest, I think he believes that when Lord Westley arrives I won't be safe somehow, because I have the same surname as his. There seems to be a feeling of hatred between the Allens here and the Westleys. Perhaps Joseph does intend to use the dynamite to blow up some dressing sheds.

"Aunt Mavis says the Westleys should be locked up in hell forever."

It had become too nerve-racking, so I reacted. "That's it. I've had enough of your ridiculous waffling. I'm not listening to you any more. I'm leaving. This place is all yours. Find your own way home."

I can't comprehend, why the town's sorry history is being dumped on me. Is it because of my surname? Perhaps it fired off the re-living of a myth of some sort? Perhaps my first guess is correct and Mike and his mates are behind it.

I do not know why, but I stayed and kept listening.

After more weaving of his dialogue about people dying, I exploded. "Joseph, stop. Your story is one you've dreamed up."

I smoothed my hand over the moss-ridden, crumbing walls of a house that could have been dynamited a long time ago. "If it's these ruins your story's about, the house had its heyday probably before you were born. It's either folklore you're playing out, by putting yourself in as the hero just to get attention, or you've got an over active imagination."

Joseph completely ignored what I said and recommenced speaking. "You've got to believe me. Lord Westley's the Evil One. I know you don't, so please, please, go see Reverend Anderson at the Church of Christian Followers in Greystone. He'll tell you it's all true, everything what I'm tellin' you."

"Why? Why should I? This Reverend you mention will only tell me you're a very imaginative boy, and your flights of fancy are limitless. You don't expect me to go and see him, now do you?"

"The parson'll tell you everything I say is true," insisted Joseph.

He'll want me to see the Governor General next, or talk to God. What a fool he's trying to make of me. The type of joke Mike would enjoy conceiving. I had been sucked into believing Joseph, although at the beginning I saw an advantage in keeping myself occupied until noon. "Go home Joseph. Leave me alone. I'll be leaving soon myself so you can wait and come with me then, if you like."

Then came the rustle of leaves. It sounded like feet moving amongst the vegetation. *Finally he's gone. Now*

I can have some peace. I was wrong. The wind had become as disturbed as it was before, arriving from some place unknown. It whined, whistled and caused banging throughout the ruins. This was joined by loud laughter, carried on the sails of the wind from some crazed soul far away. I shivered with horror.

Joseph called out in panic. "The Lord of the Manor knows I'm here early to warn you. He knows it."

"Didn't I tell you to go home?" I forced myself to dismiss that sound of maniacal laughter. *As Mike would say, there's a logical explanation for everything. I'll hold on to that thought.*

"He's coming 'cos it's the right day. If you try to leave he won't let you. Go see the parson. I don't want you to die." There was a large dose of fear in his tone of voice. Although I had gone beyond believing in him, the mad laughter in the wind was definitely not a child's creation. Even Mike could not have invented that sound.

I scrambled to my feet. I was not going to allow whoever wanted to keep the mountain to themselves, to try to scare me any longer. But my seconds of bravado were quickly over. As I stepped forward my foot slipped and sunk into something soft. What had I stood on? Was it part of a decaying body?

Jumping back, I drew my foot out of the soft goo. With shaking hand, I focused the torch light on it. I felt both relief and a desire to laugh. I had stood on the thick sandwich and fruit I had brought with me. In my awkward attempt to disengage my foot I overbalanced. On the way down a pain thumped through the side of my head. I was stunned. I blacked out for a few seconds. When back to full awareness, I scrambled to my feet. When I moved my head and back, it hurt.

"Joseph, are you still there . .Joseph?" I called, secretly wishing for no response. That would mean I had been dreaming. The more I called, the louder my words ricocheted back unanswered from the void. *Have I imagined it all, or dreamt it? Surely not.* But the question gnawed at me. I would stay no longer. *Noon be damned! I'm leaving.*

My feet moved forward, carrying me out of the ruins. I searched for the pathway; not wanting to wander too far from where I believed the track began. The last thing I needed was to become lost in this sinister place.

I quickly located the top of the downward path. I dashed down it as fast as I could manage without losing my foothold. The faster I moved, the more the shrubs and thorny bushes I had carefully rounded on the way up, seemed to want to hinder me from reaching the bottom. I pushed them desperately aside, but they switched back, belting and ripping any exposed skin. It seemed as if the distance had stretched out, to be much longer, but the overgrowth began to open up as I drew closer to the bottom, allowing me a narrow glimpse of sanctuary – the street below.

Back on the road, the thick soles of my sneakers sent a rhythmic hollow sound as I almost ran, putting the ruins and my faceless companion behind me. I was in the right frame of mind to yank Mike from his comfort zone and get the truth out of him. I would then 'throttle' him if I found he really was responsible for this hoax. If not, and it was some Rockville deranged person, the old men would know who it was. If that failed, I would put it down to delusions, perhaps alcohol and tiredness induced.

Giving it more thought, I had to admit that, if I did question Mike, I would have to tell him what I believed happened. Knowing him, he would laugh and say I was too gutless to stay until lunchtime so made up the story. The best idea was to say nothing. *If in the unlikely event that Mike is back in our room I'll tell him my watch is fast, then bore him with some inane story until he loses interest, accepts defeat, and hands over the hundred dollars.*

I was striding up to the hotel itself when I heard raised voices coming from a house on the opposite side of the street. The windows were wide open. I recognised Mike's voice ringing out over the top of the others. *He's still enjoying himself. That's good!* I looked at my watch. It showed more than half an hour was left before the deadline.

Not wanting to be recognised I circled the building until I reached the back entrance to the hotel. I crept in, hoping the clerk did not hear me. Thankfully, he was nowhere in sight. Reaching the bedroom I gently clicked the door shut behind me. I was quietly confident no one had seen me. I also knew that when Mike was enjoying himself he took no notice of time, and only moved when driven by the need for food or sleep.

. I pulled carefully at my filthy clothes, peeling them from my tired muscles. I kicked them under the bed before heading to the shower. The hot water stung as I cleaned the many scratches I had collected. I held a cold wet pad on the bump on my head in the hope it would miraculously disappear. Refreshed, I returned to my bed and gingerly climbed between clean sheets, desperate to rest in comfort. I consoled myself with the thought that the stupidity of the mountain visit was behind me, but more importantly I would be a hundred dollars richer. By returning before midday I was well aware I had lost the bet, but I told myself I had certainly earned the money. What a thrill it would be to see Mike pay out for once.

I waited until noon, then phoned the bar and left a message with the barman to tell Mike I was back. Everything remained quiet until Mike slammed the door behind him on entering our room. As I watched him stagger across the room, I could not resist a jibe. "The socializing boy's returned. The worse for wear I see."

Mike turned his blood-shot eyes in my direction." Hey Greg . . . back already? I thought you might have stayed and had lunch with the Voice on the Wind. What did you see . . . any scary ghosties?" I did not answer. That could wait.

He flopped on to the bed and began fumbling with his shoelaces. "Man, there're some weirdos around here. There was this young bloke outside in the street just now. I couldn't see him properly. He disappeared too quickly. Bit queer he was. Said he knew I was a mate of yours, and to give you an important message. 'My name's Joseph.' I think that's what he said, and to tell you not to forget what he told you about the one he wants you to see.' Got a date have you Greg, or is he the Voice, and he wants you to join him in a wind duet?"

Mike grinned with self-satisfaction at trying to stir me. Unknown to him he did, for I sat up quickly. *If he wasn't behind it, how the hell did he know the kid's name?* "How old was he?" I queried, thinking that this time I would catch him out.

Mike broke out into a fit of laughter that he obviously could not control, and splattered, "He was hiding I think, because he was gone when I turned around to face him . . . only kidding."

Why did he use the name, Joseph? I was now convinced Mike had been behind the whole charade. It had all been a set-up, his best joke yet. Before I could react angrily, he cheated me by falling spread-eagled across the bed. His loud snoring was almost instantaneous from the moment his head hit the pillow. If I woke him it would be an uphill battle getting any sense out of him. I would wait.

I lay back down on my bed. As the minutes passed I cursed not only Mike, but also a growing headache that refused to cease its pounding. *Why does he have to play his silly jokes?* I was seething as I listened to the tell-tale signs of being 'dead to the world', coming from Mike. It made my quick return to greatly needed rest almost impossible. I kept reliving what I had experienced that morning.

I wondered if what I had heard and felt in the ruins had any reality at all. I doubted Mike could have thought up most of the things Joseph had said. It was too imaginative. It would have had to come from someone else in the town. I finally concluded that Joseph was real but manipulated by others. *I'll wake Mike in a couple of hours and we'll leave. Nobody, including Mike, is going to keep me from getting out of this hole, no matter what they're planning.*

With that upmost in my mind, I became less tense. Dismissing all fearful doubts I slept.

CHAPTER 10

Mike is trapped. Greg goes for help.

Hunger awoke me from the balm of undisturbed sleep, abetted by the glare caused by the travelling sun, as its rays streamed through the lace-curtained window. Brushing back wayward strands of hair from my forehead I glanced around the room.

Realising I was still in Rockville, I was unable to curb the rising flow of memories of the ruins. I tried to tell myself it never happened, or did consuming too many beers while not having enough sleep cause a nightmare? The silent message, 'We must get out of here,' kept tapping away at my brain. I had never been truly frightened of anything in my life, so refused to accept that this feeling was anything more than nervousness triggered by what I could not give any meaning, or purpose to. But, I could not shake off the urge to be on our way and put Rockville behind us as soon as possible.

My gaze skipped over clothes I had earlier dumped in a pile on top of my overnight bag, then across to Mike. He was still deep in sleep. My head still ached, and the scratches I had collected stung as I crawled out of bed to stand beside my cousin. I bent over and shook him several times, harder each time.

Mike eventually groaned but did not open his eyes as he spoke. "Leave me alone Greg. I want to sleep. I'm expecting another late night tonight." He covered his head with his pillow.

"Oh no! You have to get up now! We're wasting time." I tried to appeal to his strong sense of punctuality.

"We've got to get going if we're to be back at College on time. There's quite a way to go yet."

"Okay, but just a few minutes more."

I walked away, knowing he was at least awake. I dragged out a clean t-shirt and jeans from my pack. I assumed an authoritative manner as I again addressed him. "I'm going to the bathroom. Be up by the time I'm finished. I want to leave this place as soon as possible, so shake a leg!" The groan he emitted, assured me he was still awake and had heard me.

After a quick shave and shower I returned to the room. As I began to gather up my personal items, I addressed Mike. "Your turn now."

Mike reluctantly rolled off his bed and grabbed his towel and fresh clothes. His thongs made a clapping sound from the wooden floor as he made his way towards the shower room.

When he returned he was still complaining. "A man must be insane to leave a nice soft bed when feeling like a good rest. But I do need some food. As my little brother always says when hungry, 'my stomach thinks my throat's cut'."

"All self-inflicted. You'll get no sympathy from me, although I agree with you about the food part." Mike flung me a look of disgust from beneath droopy eyelids. The moment to mention the bet had not yet arrived.

I finished packing and was ready to leave by the time Mike had finished getting dressed. He now looked more alive. Except for the dark patches under his eyes, all other traces of a hangover were gone. He sat on the bed and slowly pushed his belongings into his backpack.

I could wait no longer. I walked over and stood before him with my open palm up close to his chin. He frowned and stared down at it as if seeing some strange object. I make a fist. "Before you put everything away, don't forget to give me my hundred dollars . . . now." I was elated at his look of dismay.

"Ahh yes, the bet. I guess I lost, but perhaps you'd like me to hang on to it. I could use it to make a wager. I'd split the winnings with you of course. You're not lucky at gambling but I could double it for you. Naturally I'd deduct my share. I still have to pick up my winnings from Bill and the others. They had a strange idea you'd either never return, or come running back chased by some creature from hell. Charlie said you could die up there from fright. I knew better. Only the good die young I told them. Then I made a bet on it." He was trying to regain control. "Add your money to mine and I'll make us a tidy sum."

"Thanks, but no thanks . . . my hundred dollars, now!"

"Sure you won't change your mind?"

"No!"

Mike reluctantly dug into his pocket and drew out his wallet. "Ah well, I'll still be ahead. By the way, you didn't tell me about your great adventure on the hill with the Voice on the Wind. Did it come from a he or a she hiding under that bed sheet all ghosts wear?"

I grabbed the two fifty-dollar notes, folded them neatly and tucked them into my jeans' pocket. I smirked inwardly. It was not easy to get one up on Mike. I was now ready to talk, or rather, to dance around the facts. "You want to know what it was like in the ruins? Well, it was cold and dark inside the ruins. A gale-force wind accompanied by noisy surf never stopped churning out heavy metal music. I sat on hard ground and got bruises.

I lost my sandwiches, and most of my beer. It was great. You should try it some time. If you don't believe me wait 'till you see the photos I took."

"I'll take your word for it, but I did get a bit worried. You went up there to . .who knows what. There could be thugs hiding out, or wild dogs . . . anything . . . or something even worse. I did try to stop you, remember?" He seemed genuinely concerned, as I would have been for him, but I began to feel uncomfortable. It was unlike easy-going Mike to get sentimental or show regret.

"Oh yeah." I said it loudly, to cover my feelings of growing embarrassment. "You . . . worried? You were happy socializing with the locals all morning. Admit it, you weren't thinking of anything but grog and gambling."

He half smiled. "Of course I was worried to think that my friend, through no fault of mine, was bruised from sitting on hard ground in the cold and half dark, listening to a gale-force wind and the noise of a pounding surf. This friend then misplaced his sandwiches and beer in that spooky place. What a tragedy." He laughed and I grinned. Mike was back in full form.

As we were leaving the room he bowed while gesturing for me to go first through the door. "The wealthy before the good looking."

In high spirits we made our way to the dining room for a late lunch. There were no others present. The large room was furnished with four round tables, each skirted by four wooden chairs. Our waiter greeted us in a manner that suggested he was surprised to see us, and in particular, me. We sat down to enjoy a thick steak with fried eggs and a pile of vegetables. It was followed by bread and butter pudding like Grandma used to make. Mike pushed half his meal away. He continued to flood his stomach with black coffee.

The waiter handed us the menu for dinner. "Sorry." I explained. "Won't be here. We're leaving shortly."

"If you do change your mind, can I recommend the roast chicken?" *Some people just don't listen.* Mike had already picked up his bag so I quickly answered. "Okay." *What did it matter? When we don't show he'll know we've left.* We walked away with our packs slung over our shoulders.

"Greg, we may as well top up our tanks. Bill said he'd show us where the garage is. Then I have to say goodbye to the locals and collect what they owe me," Mike said as he pushed open the swinging doors into the bar. Bill was inside. We asked him about petrol and he beckoned us to follow him to a large shed. In front of it was a rusted bowser from which Bill filled our tanks.

"You can't do much business. I haven't seen any cars around," I remarked.

"We don't have any use for them now. We use the quarry bus when we need to go anywhere."

"Where do they keep it?" I had not seen or heard any bus.

Mike had begun to guide his bike towards the hotel parking area. "Come on Greg. But first there's those few outstanding wins I have to collect."

"I'll see you in the bar," Bill said as he pocketed our payments.

I followed Mike into the lounge area. He immediately went over to speak to the oldies and a couple of new faces he had met while I was up on the cliff.

Do they ever go home? I farewelled Bill, Jack and the others, and after I caught his eye, Harry. "We're off now." He came over and slapped me on the shoulder. "Why the hurry? "

"Can't be late for college." I hurried away not wishing to indulge in any discussion of my earlier sojourn.

Mike kept chatting away. The losers were amicable and parted with their money cheerfully enough. As I made a move towards the door, the old-timers lapsed into silence. They were all looking directly at me with what I interpreted as a pleading expression. It was a 'Please don't leave 'puppy-dog' look. They asked me no questions so I quickly averted my eyes. I stepped closer to Mike and nudged him. "Come on Mike. Let's get out of here. This place is weird."

"Weird . . . this one-horse town? The ruins have spooked you. As for me, except for parting with that huge amount of money to you, I've enjoyed myself."

"You always enjoy yourself when you're winning. You hated the place earlier."

Mike followed me outside where we mounted our bikes. As we drove away I was leading, with Mike following behind me. I glanced back to see him looking back and waving goodbye to some of his new friends, who were standing in the doorway returning his farewell gesture.

Turning into Rockville Road, I noticed clouds, black and menacing, were moving in from over the sea. When we drew closer to the exit that would take us to the main road intersection, wind was already blowing gritty dust on to our visors. It cut down our visibility.

The wind, which we had ignored, began to corkscrew. It became so strong we had difficultly tunnelling our way through it. I accelerated. This turned my bike into a battering ram in my effort to travel forward. *Perhaps the area is prone to twisters or those 'Roaring Forties' winds that pass through the two land masses.* But to me everything seemed out of harmony in this place. I was now even more desperate to leave it behind me.

Arriving at the exit from Rockville Road, where it joined the main road, I felt I was being drawn back. *That damn wind's trying to drag me back to Rockville.* As I accelerated further, I felt a much stronger sucking wind from the opposite direction, the way I was facing. It won, enabling me to shoot through the intersection and bounce on to the highway, almost unseating myself in the process. I was thrust into a pool of still air, in sharp contrast to what I had left behind. *This is weird?* My bike skidded on some gravel, and then turned swiftly. My boot grated along the ground to slow it down and keep my balance. The motor murmured gently as I whirled it around.

I squinted back down Rockville Road. I expected Mike to be close behind, but. he was still some distance back. He was battling that strong face-on wind, and losing. His bike had come to a standstill – its wheels spinning aimlessly. I thought for a moment that he could be swept away into the higher atmosphere, and possibly dropped out at sea.

Mike and his bike were being forced back the way we had come. I watched anxiously as Mike jumped off. He landed heavily on the ground, with his bike twisting, and then crashing down beside him. Mike squatted on the ground and shouted with his hands cupped around his mouth. "I'm okay, but I can't make it. The wind's too strong. I'll retreat to the hotel. I'll meet you there." That is what I think he said.

Although I desperately wanted to be on my way, we had to remain together. I revved the motor of my bike to rejoin Mike. It jumped forward. Its innards roared in protest as I swung to re-enter Rockville Road. As I passed the main entrance sign a sudden burst of wind slapped me unmercifully from the front. It seemed to have turned on itself. The front wheel lifted off the ground as if a giant's fingers had flicked it. I went to ground with the bike spinning in circles. I was shaken, but unhurt.

Remounting, I made several attempts to ride forward to rejoin Mike. I invited disaster each time. The wind on the Rockville side of the sign had formed an invisible wall. I could not re-enter the turn-off. Each time I barged forward, it blocked me.

I was well aware of what winds of this calibre could do, but this was beyond reason. There seemed to be two dimensions. The wind, almost non-existent on this side of the sign until I tried to join Mike, was a raging gale on the Rockville side. *I can't get back in, and Mike can't get out. There must be some sane explanation. Perhaps a channel of wind is turning back on itself when it meets the warmer currents on this main road. There seems to be two elements fighting each other. One is pushing Mike towards the sea. Another is holding me firm on this side of the sign, in a space between two opposite pushing winds. This place has made me psycho. Winds are controlled by climate not by a town. Why didn't it succeed in sucking me in with Mike?* From somewhere I heard a soft voice, 'I helped as much as I could. You must see the parson. He'll help.' I ignored it.

I continued to watch Mike. He was clinging to the trunk of a small tree with his bike lying beside him. To join him I would have to wait until there was a lull in the gale-like winds.

Out of the blue Joseph's voice came to me again. 'Go and see the parson.' I wanted to keep ignoring it, but the situation was bizarre. A twister blocked at an intersection begged a logical explanation. The urge to find out more took root. I shouted as loud as my lungs would allow. "Can't get back. I'll see you at the hotel later." He screwed up his face. I could not tell whether he heard me or not.

'Curiosity killed the cat, but information brought it back', is an old saying. It could kill me too, but anything is better than staying here and waiting for the wind to die down. I also had to admit I was curious about Joseph. W*hat's his background? Why does he say we're family? Was it because of the name Allen?* 'Not good enough.' I thought. I was very curious though. *Perhaps this Reverend Anderson, if he exists, knows the answers. Surely he would also know whether Rockville was prone to such winds. He might be able to tell me what to do if one descended the next time we tried to leave.* In my heart I did not think he would be of any help.

I viewed Mike, now standing. He had managed to right the bike and I shouted 'I'll be back soon.' He waved his hand in acknowledgement. I continued to watch him. When he mounted and faced his bike towards the town centre he seemed to have no trouble riding in that direction. The wind was almost carrying him along.

In a further attempt to rejoin Mike, I turned side-on and stretched out my arm to beyond the sign. The wind threw it back at me. *The wind seems to be keeping itself within a confined area.* It was too much for any sane man to accept. Joseph's statement regarding the parson being all-knowing came back to me. *Perhaps this Reverend Anderson of Joseph's will be able to enlighten me.* Although I believed it would be a wild goose chase, I felt I had to try. If I succeeded in finding out if these gale force winds came at regular intervals we could perhaps time it, to enable both Mike and I to get out of Rockville before tonight. *Someone must know more about this place and how to avoid the same situation again. It may just be the parson.* It seemed plausible to visit him, and see what came up. I discounted visiting the police. *What can I say to them? 'My friend got caught in a windstorm, so why didn't I? And there's a nutty kid hiding up in the ruins.'* They would probably arrest me, and throw me in the loony bin to cool off.

Still puzzled and full of unanswered questions I sped along, directing my bike towards Greystone, the closest town. I was now on a mission, to find out how to get Mike and myself out of Rockville before the end of the day. I wanted to further avoid anything that might prevent us from leaving that strange town.

CHAPTER 11

Greg goes in search for a parson.

I REACHED Greystone's main street. It was in the throes of small town activities applicable to that time of day. The few locals around were gossiping in groups, while obvious visitors were standing beside cars, licking ice creams, or sucking on soft drink bottles. I kept driving slowly as I scanned the sky over the rooftops of the shops. I was searching for a bell tower or high cross that would denote a church of some kind. If I located a church, no matter which one, people there could point me in the direction of The Church of Christian Followers.

Fifteen minutes went by and I found nothing. Was I in the wrong town? Had Joseph said Greystone, but meant Little Rock the next closest town to Rockville, in the opposite direction. After several visual sweeps, I toyed with the idea of asking directions from a shopkeeper. Before I could however, I spied a sign reading Church of Christian Followers. It was perched low on a corner post. It was what I was looking for. *If this Reverend Anderson is not a figment of Joseph's or my fantasy, he may just have the answers I want.* The thought of being stuck in Rockville forever as prisoners of a wind, made me laugh mirthlessly. 'Wild confusion' would describe my mental state, in which unsubstantiated notions continued to run riot in my head as I turned the bike into the street.

I reached an expanse of flat ground. An old sandstone church resting in wrappings of cement paths and well-cared-for grounds fronted me. At its main entrance I dismounted. I placed my helmet on the top of my bike before propping it up on its stand.

With one long leap I bounded through the front door, only to pull up sharply. The church was empty.

"May I help you?"

My body tensed. I had not heard or seen anyone enter the church. Instinctively I swung around, my fists balling, ready to face whoever had crept up on me.

"I'm sorry if I startled you. What can I do for you?"

I relaxed as I looked into the eyes of a middle-aged man, casually dressed in black slacks and white t-shirt. There was no threat from his gentle eyes and calm expression.

"I'm looking for Reverend Anderson. Is that you?'

"Oh, no, I'm Reverend Smith-James. Reverend Anderson had retired. I have taken over from him. Would I be able to assist you instead?" *There really is a Reverend Anderson!*

"Only Reverend Anderson can help, if anyone can. Where can I find him?"

"I'm afraid our dear Reverend Anderson is not much help to anyone. He's in the geriatric section of the local hospital, actually in the palliative care ward. He's not always coherent. But, if you feel I can't help you, you could speak to his granddaughter, Miss Alyce, a co-curate at this church. She is also a qualified nurse. She works at the hospital, but willingly fills in here when needed."

I was impatient to leave. With memories of the strength of the wind I had experienced at Rockville, I did not know where Mike could end up, should the wind return with the same force. I told myself that I was unduly concerned. Most gale-force winds usually exhausted themselves reasonably quickly or blew intermittently.

    Reverend Smith-James' unblinking eyes were on me. He was curious enough to want to keep talking. Strangers may pass through the town, but few would stop at a church to inquire about a former parson. I began to walk backwards, putting space between us. I had come this far and I was wasting time. The day was slipping away.

    "Are you sure I can't help?" He sounded concerned.

    "I *w*ish you could. Please, where is the hospital?"

    "The shortest way is to circle around the church building itself, and through the back gate. It's always open. Then left 'till you get to Iron Ore Street. It's the third street on the left. Swing into it and you'll see the hospital directly in front of you, and . . ."

    I was out through the door in a flash. I hastily fastened my helmet in place. I then pulled the bike off its supports, mounted, and sped past the church entrance. I glimpsed the parson at the front door shaking his head. His lips were moving and he raised his hand in a wave, or a blessing. It was impossible to tell.

    Without any difficulty I found the hospital. It was a rambling old building with added 'wings' extending out from a large round central section. These extensions would contain the hospital wards. Well-kept gardens surrounded the building. Between the arms, there were paved pathways that ended at entrances to the main central building. The grounds themselves were bounded by open land. Surrounded by serene country views it was cushioned in a bed of tranquillity.

No other vehicles were visible when I entered the hospital grounds. I parked the bike as close to the main entrance as the signs permitted, and literally jumped off. I skipped over the one step on to the patio, taking off my helmet as the glass doors slid open. My sudden entrance startled the receptionist. She looked up, but said nothing.

"Have you a Reverend Anderson here?"

"Are you a relative, a friend?"

"Neither, but it's urgent. I have to see him, talk to him."

"I'm afraid Reverend Anderson's condition is not stable enough for a discord with anyone."

I shuffled my feet. "It's very urgent . . . please." I must have sounded pathetic.

She looked thoughtful for a moment. "I'll make enquiries. Your name?"

"Greg Allen."

She rose and clip-clopped down a long corridor. I waited until she reached the junction ahead, to disappear from view. I followed silently and swiftly. At the corner I edged around the post. I saw her enter Room No. 4. It was two doors from the exit at the far end of this arm of the building. I quickly soft-shoed it back to reception. When she returned I was leaning on the counter, anxious for an affirmative reply to my request.

"His nurse said to pass on her regrets that Paster Anderson is not in any state of health to see visitors. If it's a church matter, the advice was to see Reverend Smith-James."

She read the look of dismay on my face and added. "Sorry, but I can't do anything more."

"Thanks." I walked out.

Although I had been half-hearted earlier about finding Joseph's parson, now the refusal spurred me on. I slowly rode away, bringing the bike to a halt close to the exit door. This entrance should enable me to enter and reach Reverend Anderson's room unobserved.

An almost uncontrollable urge to burst into the ward began to well up within, but I knew that nothing would be gained if hostility was created and security guards threw me out. I would only have one chance, and with several people still moving around the grounds I would have to time it right, so as not to be seen. If I could remain out of sight until there were no people in the vicinity, the parson's wing could be entered without attracting anyone's attention. If I waited out in the open I could be intercepted for loitering.

A narrow track curved and travelled around and between tall bushes that grew in the space between this wing and the next. It continued, to end at a door on the central section of the building.

Glancing around to make certain no one saw me I jumped off the bike. I wheeled it along the cement path to where, on each side, shrubs towered over me. 'A good place to hide and wait,' I thought.

I walked the bike and settled it behind some of the thick bushes where it was unlikely to be seen. I felt the bike and I were well screened but I was not over-confident. A working gardener could appear out of nowhere and ask embarrassing questions. I waited, sharp-eyed, for the coast to be clear so I could get back to the ward unnoticed.

From my cover I watched an ambulance enter the grounds and disappear from my range of vision. I drew back further when several nurses strolled by. Busy chatting, they looked neither left nor right. I heard voices and three people carrying flowers passed the entrance to the pathway. Then, nothing for some time. The grounds had become deserted.

Impatience soon got the best of me. I left the bike behind, and crept out. I walked casually, so as not to attract attention from any chance passer-by. I nonchalantly opened the back door of the wing as if I was part of the establishment. On the lookout for staff, I entered swiftly. The passageway was empty. *My luck's in.*

The knob on the door of Room No.4 turned easily and soundlessly. I slipped through and quickly pushed it shut behind me. I was instantly looking at a very attractive nurse sitting beside the bed of a very old man. His eyes were shut. She turned, obviously expecting someone else. When she realised I was a stranger, she rose in surprise. I looked into eyes of twin green pools. My heart skipped several beats. The questions in her eyes, her nervous reaction and obvious vulnerability, aroused a curious feeling within me. I wanted to protect her.

The frail, colourless, aged man in the bed broke the spell. He was squinting in concentration as he stared at me. He spoke softly. "I know you. Those strange blue eyes and hair . . . your face is familiar."

The nurse ignored him. She was frowning at me. "Who are you? What are you doing here?"

I became aware that the bed-ridden man, propped up on pillows, was trying to lean forward. I hoped he would not topple off the bed.

"Are you Reverend Anderson?" I asked him.

The nurse moved quickly to confront me. "How dare you come into my Grandfather's room without being invited. If you don't leave immediately I'll call the wardsman." *This must be his grand-daughter . . . Miss Alyve, the co-curate.*

"You must be Nurse Alyce Anderson. If that gentleman is Reverend Anderson, I would like to ask him something. It won't take up much of his time, but it's important, and urgent."

"And you are?"

"Greg Allen."

The old man, sucking in air, began to laboriously pull himself up into a sitting position with the help of an overhead ring.

"Allen, of course. I have been waiting for this for a long time Alyce. Let him talk." His voice was low, but very clear.

Alyce again ignored him and addressed me. "My Grandfather has not long to live. No one knows how he's lasted as long as he has. He has hallucinations and often lives in the past. Nothing he can say to you would be in the least bit reliable. Besides he gets very tired quickly and needs to rest."

I looked at the parson and said, "It's about Rockville. A Joseph Allen sent me."

"At last, at last." He sounded relieved as he lay back once more. "Until Joseph and the town are at rest I cannot be. Now you have come, perhaps I'll be able to die with peace in my soul. With God's forgiveness and God willing, it'll all be over soon."

Nurse Anderson placed a gentle hand on his arm. She spoke firmly. "Grandfather, you're wandering again. Joseph! Joseph! I've heard nothing but Joseph and Rockville ever since you lost Grandma Ursula. The older and sicker you get, the more confused you become. The stories you've told me exist only in your mind. The psychologist and I both know they can't be true."

She turned to face me, while moistening her bottom lip with the tip of a pink tongue. Ripples of excitement coursed through my veins. "Now Mr Allen, would you please leave!"

I could not trust myself to look for long into those soft green eyes. I could have happily moved close enough to see my face reflected in them, and stay reflected for a long time. Alyce blinked and lowered her gaze. *I must not lose track of why I'm here. It's for Mike's safety, and perhaps I'm also here for Joseph.*

Turning back to face the parson I began to feel I was wasting my time. Judging from his appearance the man could have been a hundred years old. Translucent skin was stretched tightly over his cheekbones, with the outline of his facial skeleton showing through. His eyes were sunk in valleys between eyebrows and cheekbones, while sparse white hair crowned his scalp. He looked like nothing more than a bundle of bones lying beneath the sheets. I would have to get my visit over and done with quickly.

"I won't disturb you any more than absolutely necessary. I only want to know how to get myself and my cousin Mike out of Rockville. Something like a cyclonic wind seems to be preventing us leaving together. And does Joseph really exist, or am I the victim of a hoax?"

Alyce took a step towards me. "Not Joseph again. You have to leave."

As she spoke the parson stretched out a shaky hand towards his granddaughter. "Alyce, I don't ask you for much, but I want to talk to Greg."

"As you wish Grandfather." She turned to me. "I'll give you a few minutes, but if you upset him even slightly I'll have you escorted out immediately."

"Alyce, dear child, it's all right. Come closer Greg." I stepped to the side of his bed. He continued. "Yes, you are similar. Show me your hands."

I pulled up my sleeves a short way and turned my open hands to face upward. The parson turned them over, to stare at the star birthmark above my wrist. Rarely had any one taken any interest in my birthmark, but that had changed dramatically since entering this part of the country.

"You're the first Allen with the 'Mark of the Victim' to come to see me. The others met their fate in a way I shudder to think about. Whatever Joseph has told you is true. I'm so happy to find an Allen who's listened at last. We've waited so long." He swallowed hard before going on. "Today, February 29th, is the anniversary of the disappearance of Lord and Lady Westley, gone when both their Manor House, and the town, were destroyed by Joseph in his fear of losing what he looked on as his beach only. On this day, every leap year, they return from the depths of hell to take their revenge. Joseph is powerless against this evil entity. This is what is preventing you from leaving before midnight, if at all. Joseph has given you as much assistance as he can. I know why you are here. It's to help us all rest in God's Kingdom. It's all we want, and I pray for its success. Others, with the 'Mark of the Victim' died tragically. Lord Westley still rules Rockville."

Joseph IS real! So the Westleys return from hell each leap year. Joseph said they would return tonight. This whole absurd tale can't be true. Didn't the nurse say the parson suffered hallucinations? What a tale to write up in the College mag when I get back. Here is a story worth following up. I want to know more, but has Reverend Anderson enough energy to continue.

The parson's voice rasped as he gasped for breath. "You cannot avoid going back. Lord Westley has a mania for revenge on all Allens. He seeks retribution for the destruction of his world."

Was he wandering again, as Alyce claimed he was prone to? Whichever way I looked at it, there were too many coincidences. It seemed that I could not avoid this confrontation. It appeared to me, that the parson was confirming Joseph's story. In my rational mind I could not comprehend what the parson was implying. He was convinced that the Westleys came back to this world for the sole purpose of revenge. *Is he telling me they're ghosts? And Joseph said they would return tonight.* If all this were true, ghosts can be laid to rest, with some sign language and rituals. That was my observation from films I had seen. The clergy were always the ones who had the power, and here before me was a parson of the church who seemed powerless in this instance. *But why am I involved? I don't have any powers. Am I acknowledging that ghosts exist? Mike and my parents would be in hysterics if they knew what was going through my mind at this moment.*

"Are you telling me we can't leave Rockville until after midnight, and this Lord whatsit is keeping us there, like it or not?"

"That is correct."

I was about to ask him why he called my birthmark, the 'Mark of the Victim' but Alyce intervened.

"You realise Mr Allen that all this nonsense is feeding my Grandfather's dementia."

The parson did not make any comment. He continued. "Somehow, my son, you'll be drawn to the top of the mountain tonight, the anniversary of their departure, so you must do whatever you have to do for your own protection. It will keep happening again and again . . .until the end of time . . . at four years intervals . . . at the original time of midnight, unless . . . "

"You mean I can't do anything about leaving, because two dead people are seeking revenge. That's crazy. I could keep going from here."

"You'll go back to your friend Mike. Only the outcome can change, but I have something for you. It'll protect you."

The parson half rolled around to pull a metal cross from under his pillow. It looked surprisingly heavy in his weak grip. Its two side arms were filed and sharpened to dagger sharpness. "I want you to take this cross, and don't let it out of your possession. When you see Joseph be sure to have it with you. Whatever you do tonight you must keep it with you. Use it when you have to. When you walk through the Valley of Death fear no evil." I felt I must humour the man, so with a straight face, I took the cross from his outstretched hand.

Worry lines crossed the concerned face of Alyce, who had been standing back and wringing her hands. "See what he's done to that cross. He carries it around with him all the time. No one has ever been able to take it from him. He stresses out if anyone tries. Now he hands it over to you, a stranger. Of course what he's telling you is a figment of his imagination, a distortion of his feeble mind."

"I'm inclined to agree. I have every intention of getting out of Rockville as soon as I retrieve Mike."

I looked back and addressed the parson. "Will this cross get us both out?" I asked. In normal circumstances I would have guffawed at the mere suggestion of a cross stopping a wind, a voice, a ghost, a demon or whatever from some other dimension. That was for entertainment purposes only. *I'm now as mad as the rest in this nightmare.*

"The Westleys will not let you leave. But you are Joseph's, and the town's, only chance now. You are . . ." He started to cough.

"That's quite enough." Alyce pushed herself between the bed and me – her body brushing against mine. I had a sudden urge to kiss her as I swung from the thought of a possible death warning, to the excitement of being near her. *What is happening to me?* She went on talking. "If the cross is what you came for, have it. Go! You can see Grandfather is too old and ill for any more conversation. If I'd known you were going to discuss this Joseph, who has haunted him since Grandma Ursula died tragically all those years ago in Rockville, I'd have stopped this nonsense in the beginning."

I glanced at the Reverend to gauge his reaction, but his eyes were closed. "All right I'm going, but I hope this works."

Alyce spoke to me as if addressing a child. "I am versed in God's ways. I am a curate at His church. That cross has been blessed. It will protect you in whatever you are up to." Alyce was now ambivalent.' It seems you also are caught up in the supposed mystery of Rockville. Believe me, there's no such thing. There never was. An accident happened there years ago in which Grandma died. That's all."

I could do nothing else but leave, and take the cross with me. Things were getting too deep for me. I gave the parson a parting glance. He opened his eyes and whispered, "Alyce."

"Yes Grandfather?"

"Give this to Greg." The parson's hand had closed over a small bottle on his bedside table. "It's Holy Water Greg. You'll know what to do with it when the time comes."

Holy Water . . . the water blessed by priests and such clergy! Bemused, I accepted the bottle from Alyce. Our hands touched.

The parson leaned over on to one elbow. "Alyce, you know that sealed envelope in the top drawer of the cabinet. I want to give it to Greg. It'll explain . . ." He stopped, again struggling with his breathing.

"That envelope you've been carrying around all these years? I always thought it contained personal papers. If it's anything to do with your hallucinations, the sooner it's gone the better." Alyce opened the drawer of the bedside cabinet and drew out a large envelope, now yellow with age. Its edges were bent and roughened from much handling. Her Grandfather took it in shaking hands and pushed it along the bed in my direction.

This was becoming too much for me. I backed away. "Look, this has gone far enough. I'm only here to find out how to get myself and Mike out of that nightmare of a town, should there be any more unexplainable obstructions."

The parson spoke again, softly at first, then louder as he forced air in and out of his lungs. "I'm the only one who can dispatch all to their eternal rest. I'll be waiting for you to come for me tonight, but remember, it will happen at midnight so I have to be at Rockville before then."

Alyce's testy voice followed me as I turned to leave. "You see what's you've done. He's wandering again. Please go and don't come back."

I knew I had disturbed her greatly, and I had an urge to stroke her face as she marched towards me. I backed out the door to avoid her walking into me. I would be glad to get away from the raving man, but I would miss leaving the presence of the lovely Alyce. I was smitten.

CHAPTER 12

Greg's decision is fraught with great danger.

I PROPPED the Holy Water into the top pocket of my shirt the moment I was outside, and self-consciously pushed the cross down inside the front of my jacket. I kept my body rigid, hoping I did not pierce myself.

I felt foolish when I mounted the bike with my jacket bulging with a cross and a pocket full of Holy Water. Mike would laugh himself silly if I told him about this, but he would not be hearing it from me.

Damn! I've left the envelope behind . . . probably for the best. I don't want to know what's in it. I already have the feeling I'm being nudged into something I'll most likely regret. Hopefully, by the time I get back, the wind will have returned to wherever it came from, and Mike and I can leave. I've had enough of this nonsense.

On my journey back to Rockville I tried to analyse what had taken place in Room No. 4. I had hoped that Reverend Anderson would give me a simple explanation that I could relate to. Instead, he wanted me to believe that a demon from hell, or whatever else Lord Westley was called, returned on the 29th February in every leap year. Ridiculous as it seemed, this year's events seemed to involve Mike and me, especially me. *Why?*

I was also amazed at the parson's support of Joseph. At the same time I had to accept that he was a very old man. According to Alyce, he was subject to flights of fancy. I had to take what he said with a grain of salt. Had I attempted to get more concrete information, Alyce would have stopped me seconds after I began.

The heat of the cross began to scorch my skin, although it was not a hot day. I was tempted to toss it into some bush on the side of the road. It was only metal and could not be of any great value, but I did not want to waste a second by slowing down. I was in a hurry to get back to Rockville and collect Mike. I was no longer expecting any further obstacle to prevent us leaving.

I drifted back to thinking of Alyce. Something had drawn me to her from the instant we met. With her neat well-proportioned figure, flawless skin and quiet assurance, she reminded me of a painting of a ballet dancer in the university library. *Perhaps it's fate ... Huh ... rubbish! She'd be no different from any other girl I've dated.* But, in my heart I knew she was someone special. *Hold it! I've got more pressing things to think about than drool over some girl I don't know, and not likely to see again. Of course, I could return the cross on our way through Greystone later today. It would be a good excuse to see her again. She'd be pleased. She gave me to understand her Grandfather was very attached to it.* I shook off the vision of her sweet face, to cast my mind back to the more pressing things before me.

Engrossed as I was with those tumultuous thoughts, it seemed but a short time before I reached the Rockville turnoff. Apprehension set in as I slowed my bike at the intersection, but as I entered Rockville Road still air cloaked me. *Is the cross working? Stupid thought ... probably the wind's dropped. They never go on forever. I should have waited and not bothered with the parson.*

I was still determined to leave as soon as possible. Daylight had begun to fade. Speeding past the 'Welcome' sign, I brought the bike to a standstill in front of the Hotel.

Hurrying inside I literally flew upstairs. I was relieved. The room was empty. I hid the cross under my pillow. I wanted to avoid Mike's ridicule. He would tell everyone at college that I intended to become a priest, or had joined some sect. What a joke that would be.

It was not that I did not go to church occasion-ally, but my generation tends to query all things that you cannot see, feel, or have no scientific explanation attached to them. Nevertheless I accepted my parents' faith and carried it on. Perhaps that is why I accepted the cross without protest. But did such faith as the parson's have enough power to combat whatever evil force he believed operated in Rockville? In the parson's belief in a revengeful lord, this cross was very important in whatever game they seemed to be playing. I did not understand what it was, and did not wish to know what it was.

I found Mike fronting the bar counter downstairs. It was very noisy. More people were present, in contrast to the previous occasion. Small groups of people were seated towards the back of the room, while others were milling around. Mike was drinking with a man who looked like a human tank. He was big, dark-haired, and had a European appearance.

I'll have to persuade Mike to leave with me soon, so we're well away from here before dark.

Mike straightened up when he saw me. "Hi Greg, it's about time. I've been wondering where you were. I've . . ." He suddenly broke off to include the man beside him. "Meet Pete. He and Mavis came in a little while ago." *Not Joseph's Aunt Mavis and friend Pete? It can't be. If it* were, I was right. There was a Joseph alive and well, and prone to telling tall stories. I was set at ease by the thought that the mystery was soluble at least to my satisfaction.

"Glad to meet you." I eagerly shook Pete's hand. The coldness of it shocked me. The roaring wood, burning in a fireplace with glittering brass surrounds, was dispatching warmth to every corner of the room. Its flames rose hot and bright as if from sun-soaked desert sand. I felt too warm in my leather jacket. I spoke quietly to Mike. "Let's go Mike. Let's get out of here. This place freaks me out."

"Greg, what's the rush? We still have plenty of time before we're expected back at college. Come on, don't be a party pooper, have a beer."

"I don't want a beer. We're better off out of here before you've had too much to drink. There's more to this place than meets the eye. You wouldn't believe what I've been through." I knew he would not, and I had no intention of enlightening him.

"Did that big bad wind get to poor Greg? I found it quite exciting. Apparently that sort of thing is common here. It's the way the winds are channelled between land, mountains and high cliffs. Anyway, I can't go 'till tomorrow. I've a date tonight. I met this chick. She's Harry's niece. She said she'd be back later. You'll meet her, but remember, I saw her first."

"There'll be girls in the next town, or the one after that." I looked around. "Why all the people? What's going on?"

"They came in early and farewelled some church bloke, who's transferred to some other town. Some of them are still hanging around. I think the whole town'll be here soon. Some kid's lost. Apparently he has a habit of wandering off and scaring people. His Aunt Mavis and Pete are worried. They plan to organise a search party. I might go with them."

For some reason, I could not bring myself to tell them that Joseph had spoken to me on the mountain. Now I knew Joseph was real, a picture formed in my mind. *Joseph is found. He'll appear here later, and pretend he's never seen me before. It will all be a happy ending.* But something disturbed me to the extent that, without thinking any deeper, I blurted out. "You mustn't go with them Mike. I can't tell you why, because I don't really know myself, but the only place I want you to go is out of here, with me now."

"Greg, just think about it. We'll have to pack up. Then we must have a farewell drink with our new friends. Then there's the hassle of finding somewhere to stay in Greystone or the next town overnight. Harry said there's not much back-packer's cheap accommodation around either. I say we stay here. I promise I'll leave as early in the morning as you want, although around lunchtime would be best." He looked at my face, read behind the deep frown, and added hopefully, "That's if I have a choice."

"You haven't!"

Pete interrupted, looking at me with a half-pleading expression. "Why not leave Mikey alone. We been enjoy his company. It long time since we had such, what you say, con . . . genial company. Let him finish his drink. Then you come, meet Mavis. You hungry? The food' here's good."

Knowing it was useless to try and persuade Mike further at that time, I muttered. "Looks like I'm outnumbered." I would try again later. Some instinct again warned me not to stay the night for the sake of solving some mystery surrounding Rockville. I was in no mind to try to find out whether any of those inane forecasts I had been deluged with, would become a reality. Strangely, this was against my usual insatiable curiosity.

Mike picked up his glass and I followed him to Pete and Mavis' table. Mavis wore a loose old-fashioned floral dress. I only noticed it, because my mother had a similar dress once. Pete did not sit down. He introduced us, slowly emphasising her last name and mine, 'Allen'. Hearing my name, her large eyes lit up as her narrow lips twisted in a smile so sweet I stared in surprise. When I bent towards the grey-haired lady, I looked into a dry face of wrinkles and sadness. I muttered, "It's a common name." It was all I could think of saying.

Mike did not sit down. He smiled at Mavis. "I'll be up at the bar with Pete. We'll join you two later."

Mavis make no comment, and continued our conversation. "Allen is not a common name in these parts. At the moment, there's just me. I married an Allen, and of course there's my nephew Joseph. Other Allens have come and gone. Now you're here."

"I'm passing through as well. Mike and I were leaving this afternoon but Mike wants to stay longer, so he's stalling."

"Passing through? We pray that will be so." *Do they want us to leave? Are we distracting them from their day-to-day pattern of living?* "Sit here next to me," invited Mavis.

My bare arm brushed hers as I sat down. "Sorry." I pulled my arm away. I had discarded my jacket because of the warmth in the room. Her flesh was cold. I was as surprised as when I shook hands with Pete. *Perhaps I have a fever of some sort. Hell no! Going down with something could keep me in this creepy place longer. I wouldn't trust a doctor who practised here.*

Mavis was now looking at me with such intensity I was becoming embarrassed. "You have the Allen's shade and style of hair and the same cornflower blue eyes." *Not again!*

"Do you want to order?" Pete had returned and was leaning over the table towards me. "There's only one set meal, sort of stew thing 'cos most of the town's here and more coming, so the cook make easy food ready. I go get for you both. Mavis can keep you, our new friend, company." My skin for some reason was turning into a mass of goose bumps. *Friends in this town? That I don't need.* "Won't be long time." Pete was gone.

I stayed quiet, hoping Mavis would turn to another subject, but no such luck.

"Did you see anyone in the ruins this morning?" she asked. *The whole town must be discussing my stupidity in going up an unsafe mountain road in a strong wind on a bet.* "I believe there was a young boy," I answered reluctantly.

"Blond hair, blue eyes like yours?"

"I don't know. I didn't' see him. He kept hiding and I couldn't spot him." I did not want to discuss it further. I would have liked to tell Mavis that Joseph believed he had, or is going to, cause destruction somewhere in the cove. Somehow, I could not find the words. It could upset her if I, an outsider, told her the boy was talking as if he was off his brain. I also did not know if Mike could overhear our conversation, although I doubted it would be anything. He was now in deep conversation with a petite blonde at the next table.

Mavis interrupted my train of thought.

"Joseph keeps running away ever since he heard the parson was leaving. He was like a father to Joseph. Some of the town's people are getting ready to find volunteers to go looking for him. The parson's wife's also very worried about Joseph. She's still in town. She stayed behind to finish packing and make the house spotless for the new pastor. She'll be here soon," Mavis said

What further proof did I need that Joseph was flesh and blood, and not a spectre of the parson's dementia, or some nightmare of mine? I was at a loss. I knew where he was, and I felt she too would have realised he was hiding in the ruins. Obviously no one had gone up there and brought him back home. They would have needed only one or two who knew him well. I thought of Pete. *This place gets stranger by the minute.* I willed Pete to hurry. Hopefully his presence would change the topic of conversation, but he was still in line waiting for our meals.

"You must go back and talk to Joseph. He'll listen to you." Her eyes were pleading, distress filled.

"Go back there again! Definitely not!" was my instinctive response. *Once up there was more than enough.*

"You must, Greg. You can get him to come home and stay here where he belongs. I know it."

He wouldn't leave earlier, when I asked him to. He even got upset. "Why me, a stranger? Why not someone from the town, like Pete, his idol? And there's the search party. They should be able to find him and bring him home."

"None of us can get to him. He becomes elusive, and in turn keeps us here in a vacuum. You're an Allen, real family. You can persuade him to come home. "

"But we are not related, or I'd have known."

Pete had returned. *What a lucky break.* "Here's your meal Greg. You lucky fellow, no beef stew for you. The dining room waiter bring this. He say you order earlier. Here's sauce, Anglo, tomato?"

It was what the waiter had coerced me to pre-order, roast chicken and a mixture of roasted vegetables. He obviously used his sixth sense, or good guesswork, to know we would not be leaving early, as planned.

"'Thanks Pete." I really meant 'thanks for cutting off my discourse with Mavis.'

I ate in silence while they both watched me. It was unnerving. Why such surveillance? I wiped some gravy from the side of my mouth and pushed the empty plate away. *Now I must persuade Mike to leave. I'm getting jittery around these people.*

The instant she realised I was endeavouring to stand, Mavis placed her cold hand on my arm, restraining me, "Don't go yet. Pete, tell him." Pete nodded. I reluctantly settled back down again.

"Joseph and you have got same kinda hair and eyes of the other Allens. Something else, Mavis say Allens have some mark on body."

I had turned my hand face-up several times so they could not have failed to see the birthmark above my right hand. I was about to mention that, but instead I said, "I suppose you're going to tell me that all Allens are born with similar birthmarks."

Mavis answered. "Not all. I believe it's only males born into one branch of the Allen family. I'm not certain how often this happens. As far as I know no females have the mark." *Could it be possible that I'm related to these Allens? No! My father would have told me to call on them on the way home.* "As an Allen you're the only one who can help Joseph. You'll be a substitute for the family he misses, so he'll co-operate with you. Tonight, Evil Ones will be stalking the mountain. Joseph needs your help."

"Evil Ones?" It was becoming eerie again. Did she mean vandals and no-hopers?

"Call it gossip, or folk lore if you want to, but I beg of you. Please Greg, go to him. Help him and do a great kindness for us all."

I did not want a repeat of the morning's traumatic experience, but my heart resonated with compassion. Mike always said I was a sucker for a hard luck story. Surely it would have been better for Mavis and Pete to go to him. She was his aunt and should be able to talk him into coming home. I did not suggest it as I felt her answer would be one I would not be able to counter.

Joseph wouldn't leave this morning with me, but should he be in the same friendly mood I may get through to him. He must want something to eat by now. Before I realised it, I heard myself saying. "I'll go, but he mightn't listen to me."

Mavis took my hand in her still icy one and kissed it. "I feel that you'll succeed Greg, but say nothing to anyone, especially to Mike. Remember, you must leave the top of the mountain before midnight. Midnight is." She stopped abruptly and compressed her lips as Pete put his arm around her shoulders.

That midnight time-scale again. "I'll make a quick trip. It'll be up to Joseph. If he refuses to come back with me, I'll leave him there and come back alone. *I certainly won't tell Mike, the sceptic, what I'm planning. He'd rightly tell me I was out of my mind.*

"You don't know how happy this makes us. God bless and protect you." Tears were glistening in both her eyes.

Picking up my jacket I stood up and said. "I'm off then, before it gets any later."

I left the table and stopped beside Mike who had moved his chair closer to the blond girl. "I'm going to bunk down for a while," I lied. "We're getting up at the crack of dawn, so don't forget." *Where has my determination to leave Rockville before nightfall, gone?*

"You're getting soft Greg. You're going to miss a party we've been invited to. I'll just be in the swing of things around then."

"Too bad. Dawn it's going to be." I escaped before he could argue further.

I planned to be back in a few hours. Perhaps less, if I located Joseph quickly, and he was co-operative . . . perhaps two if he wasn't. That would be well before midnight. *Why does everyone mention midnight?* I let this thought sink to the bottom of my mind.

Back in my room I flopped on to the bed. I would rest for a bit before tackling the long walk up the mountain again. Unbidden, Alyce's face appeared before me.

I felt a strong urge to see her. *When we reach Greystone tomorrow I'll stop at the hospital and hope she's on duty. I can't return home without seeing her again.*

Unintentionally I dozed off.

A noise, or was it a voice calling my name that woke me. I assumed I must have been dreaming, as I heard nothing more. My watch showed 10 p.m. I had delayed much longer than intended. Mavis would have expected me to be back with Joseph in tow before now. I would have to hurry. Once on my feet I stretched. My neck had a kink in it. *The cross*! I had slept with the cross under my pillow. I pulled it out and looked at it. *Create a miracle? That's ridiculous. I certainly won't be using it for anything. But better please the old man, and perhaps this would please Alyce. Coming from the parson the cross could be an enticement for Joseph to return home. It'd be proof that his parson is looking out for him. In this place I'm beginning to believe anything ridiculous is possible.*

I dressed, putting on my padded leather jacket and long thick pants for warmth. I hesitated over taking the phial of Holy Water, but then slipped it into my shirt pocket. It would be something else for Joseph. The cross I stuck in at an angle between my shirt and wide leather belt. I felt the pointed arms would be less likely to annoy me there than down my shirt. I buttoned up my jacket. The cross was now out of sight. Ready to leave, I searched for my small torch but could not find it. Not wanting to waste any more time I went to Mike's bag and seized his larger torch. It had a stronger beam than mine.

No one was in the street as I left the hotel. I glanced back through one of its windows. It was more crowded now. A man was standing, giving some sort of talk. Not wanting to be seen and asked questions, I walked in the shadow of any tree I came to.

I had no trouble finding steps up the mountain, but I noticed they were blocks of stone. *How did I miss the overgrown half-broken concrete and earth ones?* It did not matter. It was still a path to the top.

I tried to ignore rustling in the bushes and a loud squawk from what I hoped was only a frightened sea bird. No one had mentioned any wild animals about these parts, so I did not dwell on such possible risks. Nothing else disturbed me. I felt I had been drained of any nervous reaction to the unknown by my previous sojourn and the events that followed.

On reaching the top I was forced to bend almost double as I moved forward beneath the low branches blocking my path. Suddenly I stopped and caught my breath. I was facing an ornate gate. Hesitating briefly, I pushed it open and walked through. I hurried on until I rounded a thick bush. As I did, I was transfixed. Like a mirage, a house, the size of a mansion had materialised before me. It was nestled in an obviously well cared-for garden. *The manor house . . . am I lost? Impossible! I've merely bypassed the track to the ruins. It must be close. To save time looking for it, I'll see if anyone's home. If there is, I'll ask them if they know Joseph's whereabouts. If not, I'm sure they'll direct me to the ruins.*

CHAPTER 13

Greg faces the death reaper.

I STOOD in awe for some time. When I decided I was not imagining things, I pulled out my camera. I took several photos, hoping there was enough light to show the manor in all its grandeur. I then followed a cobblestone path that serpented its way through the immaculate garden. My amazement grew as more of this Georgian style mansion came into view. It had so many different facets of skilfully created artwork in timber and cement. I was loath to move towards its colourfully lit entrance, before I absorbed more of its beauty. *So this is what Joseph meant when he said I would see the Manor House tonight? This is better than mouldy old ruins. But where is Joseph? Perhaps he intends to meet me here.*

    A light shining through an open window got my attention. As I drew closer to it, girlish laughter assailed my ears. It had a seductive ring to it. I knew I should not approach the window. It would be unethical and against the training that had shaped my upbringing. If caught I could be accused of spying by some enraged lover/husband, to whom I assumed the lady was directing all her attention. That was not a comfortable thought, and besides, I was on a mission to locate Joseph. I refused to look either right or left, but the delicate chiming of bell-like laughter grew louder. My senses clamoured to seek out its source. I moved closer to the window, but guilt made me step back. I hesitated before taking another step in that direction.

"Get away!" The voice was behind me. Startled, and with the feeling that an icy hand was tickling my spine I swung around. It was a young boy.

"Joseph?"

"Yes."

"You're an expert at frightening people. I didn't hear you coming." I was looking into a sad limp face. It was true he had eyes the colour of mine, and the same unruly fair hair.

"Did you see Reverend Anderson?" His voice sounded anxious.

"Yes, but he's an old feeble man."

"I know. Did he tell you everything 'bout me?"

"Well, I'm not sure . . . no . . . not really. He was wandering in his mind and speech, but he did beg me to come and find you. He said I had to get you off the mountain somehow. Everyone seems to think, because we're both Allens, I would succeed. The parson also thinks we're related like you said, but it's farcical to even consider it. I'd have known."

I unbuttoned my jacket and tapped the cross now showing behind my belt. "He gave me a gift for you," I lied, but it seemed the best way to handle things. If he thought the parson was still interested in his welfare I would probably be able to get him back to his aunt. "If you won't come back with me I'll leave it with you, and be off." He stepped back so I rebuttoned my jacket.

"You'll stay, and you must keep the Holy Water with you. *How does he know I have some?* I was beyond trying to come up with an explanation that made sense. "Either come with me now or I leave without you," I repeated.

"Lord Westley won't let you leave."

I was not getting my message across. I had merely started Joseph running amok again with his story telling. I was on the verge of forcing the cross and the Holy Water on him and leaving, but before I could act, the tinkling laughter assailed my ears again. It seemed closer. It drenched my senses. I forgot Joseph, and was ready to explore the possibilities it implied. I wanted to see her; meet her.

In my state of being sleep-deprived earlier in the day, I had been unable to absorb everything Joseph had rambled on about. But, I did recall that the house would be destroyed somehow. I was convinced that he was some sort of schizo. He had expressed his hate for the Westleys most profoundly. So, why was he still here, walking beside me? I halted, wanting confirmation. "This is the Westley's place isn't it . . . the Manor House you told me about?"

"Yes."

"You said something about causing an explosion? I knew you were lying. Where are the ruins?"

"The ruins are here."

"Show me."

"Not now. I can't."

I wanted to take him by the scruff of the neck and shake him to get at the truth. *If it weren't for the parson and the hope of bringing some peace to him in his last days I'd be out of here.* But it was not the parson I was concerned about. It was Alyce.

Ahh well. I'll dispose of the parson's cross and the Holy Water at the first opportunity, and then get back, with or without Joseph. You can't win 'em all. But first I must get a glimpse of the one with a laugh that promises a glimpse of heaven.

The appealing laughter signalled to me again. It caused my skin to creep as if covered by a hundred marching ants. I turned my gaze once again towards the window. Inside was the source.

Joseph linked his arm through mine and held tight, determined to stop me advancing any further towards the window. I conceded. We walked on. I was happily thinking that we were now nearing the entrance to the house. I felt that I would soon meet the woman with the sea siren's song of promise. As we moved forward, other niggardly thoughts entered my mind. I was still puzzled, and still wanted answers. I asked Joseph. "If I remember correctly, you claimed Lord Westley is evil and wants to kill me, but you're going with me to his home . . . why?"

"I'm not taking you. Lady Westley is sucking you in." *More lies.* But why Joseph was accompanying me when he supposedly hated the owners was beyond my comprehension. I thought it would be the last place he would want to be.

Joseph gripped my arm more tightly. "Come away," he demanded, tugging at me. I tried to jerk my arm away, but he still held his grip. I almost dragged him with me on to the patio, to face the front door, on which a glittering brass lion's head took pride of place. The top jaw formed an umbrella over a large knocker from where it emitted light in rainbow hues, and giving out welcoming vibrations.

The heavy solid wooden door opened the instant we stood before it. Joseph dropped my arm as I managed to pull away from him and enter. Inside I paused. From behind a closed door on my right, flowed another fountain of bewitching laughter. Joseph closed in, this time blocking my path, obviously determined to guard me against temptation. I walked around him, into the lounge area. I began to wonder why I had come inside. We had not been invited. Would the owners be annoyed and order us to leave?

Bewitching perfume now billowed around me, coming from behind. I turned quickly, to be transfixed at the sight of the most beautiful woman I had ever seen. She had the flawless face and figure of my little sister's beloved doll 'Lady'. Her long black hair cascaded around her shoulders and down her back, emphasising the white skin of her face and neck. Her body enthralled me. It was an hourglass figure, dressed in a flowing, floating sea of soft silky fabric covered with peepholes of lace. Her whole being radiated youthful unspoiled beauty and freshness. Her smile and the innocent expression in the smiling eyes captivated me. I moved towards her.

"Greg . . . no!" It was Joseph's voice.

I came back to reality, noticing for the first time a man entering the room. He came to her side, and then bowed to me. His manner was that of a charming, cultured gentleman. *Her husband?* I shivered. Was it from jealousy, or something else?

"I am Lord Flurice Henry Argyle Westley. I see you have become acquainted with my lovely wife, Lady Phoebe. And you are?"

"Greg Allen."

"Greg Allen, of course. Forgive me. We are always happy to welcome any Allen to our modest abode." *Something else Joseph lied about.* Lord Wesley waved his arm, indicating he wished me to go through a carved archway into another room. "Be my guest. Come, we will be much more comfortable at the bar." Joseph was not included in the invitation. He did not even warrant a glance.

Curious, I crossed over the carpeted floor whose pile gave a springy feel to my feet. Joseph still lagged behind. Amazed at the opulent interior, I straggled along behind Westley, into what looked to be the main lounge. It was a room elegant in its tasteful choice of furniture and décor. It was English period furniture. The paintings depicted people in attire, both past and present. *If this man is a demon from hell as they claim, I'm a monkey's uncle.*

At Lord Westley's invitation, I followed him into what appeared to be where he entertained his guests. We stopped at an elaborately carved bar, made from Huon Pine. It had a two-seater armchair and a single-seater facing it. There were dark stains on the headrest and I wondered why they did not get one of their staff to remove them. *They must have plenty.* Apart from that, I noticed little else. I was faced with the choice of forcing the parson's items on Joseph and leaving quickly, or lingering in the hope of getting to know the living, breathing vision before me.

Lord Westley stopped in front of his well-stocked hand-carved bar. I stood beside him, intrigued with the rows of expensive wines and liqueurs. These people oozed wealth from every pore. Lady Westley had crept to my side unnoticed, but Lord Westley intervened and guided me to the lounge chair facing the bar. His wife was already seating herself.

"Won't you sit down there beside my Lady?"

'Heaven could not have granted me a better wish,' I thought. This chair also had dark stains on the fabric, but I was too entranced to be concerned with such details. As I seated myself beside Lady Phoebe I was aware of the memory of her haunting, tinkling, laughter. She pressed her warm body against mine and I felt bewitched.

Lord Westley acknowledged Joseph's presence for the first time. "Joseph, how pleased we are that you are with us. A drink for another Allen would be in order, don't you think?" he hissed. Until Westley spoke I had forgotten Joseph. I looked around. He was standing under the nearest archway. He wore a forlorn expression on his face.

"No!" Joseph was empathic in his response. "He don't want your drink."

I can speak for myself. "Of course I'll have a drink." Anything to delay leaving. *I can't possibly leave without hearing Lady Phoebe's voice. Will it be as seductive as her laugh?*

Joseph, who had been hanging back, as if not wanting to come close to the Westleys, now ran behind the bar. He quickly took a bottle of soft drink from one of the shelves. He poured some of its contents into the glass Lord Westley had placed ready for me. He handed it to me. Westley watched, looking amused.

"You are slick tonight Joseph, but all to no avail I'm afraid." His short high-pitched laugh of contempt made me squirm. I knew that Joseph hated the Westleys, and the one-upmanship Lord Westley was playing, revealed that the deep hate was mutual. Perhaps, as the parson said, it was a vendetta against Joseph, and by association, all Allens. I tried to recall everything Joseph and the parson had told me, but my thoughts had become too distorted in my memory to retrieve clearly. I wondered why Lord Westley did not tell him to leave or why Joseph stayed around. Perhaps he was too simple to fully understand the depth of the hate, or, was he intimidated by the Westleys, but at the same time fascinated?

Lord Westley lifted his own full glass and waved it before him. Joseph had now retreated, to stand near the entrance. Westley raised his voice. "Revenge is sweet. Sometimes I think the apostles had the Westleys in mind when they wrote. 'Revenge is mine, saith the Lord.' It is indeed, for this lord."

Joseph was watching me with concern. He continually wrung his hands. I felt that the hate expressed by Westley for Joseph excluded me, as I found the Westleys to be the essence of Old World charm.

"Perhaps you'd like a different drink Greg, from me, not from a child. I will pour you a man's drink." He put out his hand, took away the glass I was holding, and handed me a freshly filled one. Before Joseph could interfere I had taken several gulps. I was not accustomed to drinking liqueur, but the mixture of spice, sweetness, and the satin feel of it going down my throat made me want more. I took another one. Joseph was shaking his head with dismay. I put the glass down, perplexed.

Lady Phoebe drew closer. Her hand now rested on my knee. "You are very handsome," she crooned. She tilted her head to one side exposing her white neck. My stomach made a somersault. I felt she wanted me to kiss her there, and the eagerness to comply was building within me when Joseph spoke again.

"Leave him alone!" The mood was broken. *Why is the kid interfering?*

"She's only having fun," her husband pointed out, with an accompanying smile filled with malice towards Joseph.

Joseph responded angrily, "Leave him alone! You got the others. You can't have him too." *Have me? What for?* A haze was descending before my eyes. Perhaps the drink was stronger than I thought. I pushed it away.

"He's family, and my friend too. Aren't you, Greg?"

"Of course." *Why argue?* I thought of the parson and was about to say something featherbrained like; 'Any friend of the parson is a friend of mine', but the tearful expression on Joseph's face stopped me.

Lady Phoebe's cheek was now lightly touching mine. I felt cool softness. I inhaled the intoxicating aroma of her perfume. My emotions were starting to struggle and win against common sense. The situation was threatening to get out of control. That knowledge did not destroy the growing desire in me to be closer to her, like a hungry child drawn to its mother's breast.

"Drink up Greg. There's plenty more, and the night's young."

"Don't Greg! You must stay cool. These people are evil." *Evil? Beautiful you mean.*

I blinked a few times to try to take away a sudden blurriness. I knew then my drink had been spiked. Lord Westley strolled to the back of the chair; standing directly behind me. I was too vague mentally to query this strange behaviour.

I was gazing like a lovesick teenager into Phoebe's eyes when a hand suddenly gripped my longish hair from behind, drawing my head backwards, imprisoning it against the high padded headrest. Joseph's voice screamed through my head. "Greg, move!"

Grabbing Westley's wrist with one hand I flung myself forward and upright, out of the chair. I twisted my body around trying to directly face the now distorted demonic face of Lord Westley. His hold on my hair tightened. I felt that at any moment each strand would be dragged painfully from my scalp. I was groggy, disorientated, and my limbs felt limp and lifeless. I tried to pull away. I tried to concentrate, to focus, to diminish the effects of whatever had been put in my drink. I tried to push him away with both hands, but my gestures lacked force. The world had become dream-like.

Westley gave a hollow, chilling laugh as Lady Phoebe, now beside her husband, drew a dagger from within the folds of her gown. I watched in a vague disinterested way. Her husband's hand closed over its handle. My head was jerked back further. Horror-stricken I watched the blade descending, directly in line with my eyes. My forearm flung upward instinctively to ward it off. It had little weight behind it but it knocked Westley's hand away. The knife missed my face and descended towards my upper arm. It punctured my leather jacket, piercing my arm with a stinging jab.

The instinct to survive heightened my reflexes. Before Westley recouped for a second attempt, I twisted my body around as far as I could. I gripped the wrist of the hand holding my hair. I dug my nails into the veins with as much strength as I could muster, and scraped. He released my hair. I tried to jump away, but something was blocking me. It was Lady Phoebe. Her face had changed and now mirrored the vile expression of her husband. Where was the doll-like visage with the pert lips? The staring eyes were the glistening black circles of a she-devil. The corners of her lips were turned down in a fiendish sneer.

I tried to steady myself but in that split second of hesitation, Phoebe moved like a cat, gripping my arms from behind, and pinning them to my side. I struggled to free them but her size belied her strength, and in my weakened state I failed.

Westley moved in closer as Phoebe pushed me towards the chair. I was still trapped. "Thank you my dear. He wriggles so, does he not?"

The lock of her arms was not strong enough to hold me indefinitely. I tried to elbow myself out of Lady Phoebe's grip, preparing to defend myself, but, distracted by a low growl, I hesitated again. A large fierce guard dog was bounding towards me, teeth bared. Another followed. Phoebe pushed me down into the chair. At the same time Lord Westley was again positioning the knife above my face. Panic gripped me – adrenalin pumped. Lord Westley laughed a blood-curdling laugh and faced towards Joseph. 'How do you like this Joseph?" There was silence. Westley lowered the knife, holding it away from the front of my face.

In that tiny space of wasted time on my part when I could have made a move against Phoebe, Westley produced a length of rope. He formed a lasso. Phoebe immediately stepped to one side. Grinning with self-satisfaction Westley deftly swung the rope from one hand. It circled both the chair and me, binding me to it. He drew the rope tight, frustrating any further efforts on my part, to escape.

"Rustus, Queenie, guard him," Phoebe ordered. The dogs crouched down. Their bodies were poised to attack on command.

Phoebe fumbled with the cord ends in an effort to fasten the rope tightly, but by tensing my body it was looser than she intended. Nevertheless any possibility of protecting myself from Westley and the dogs now appeared hopeless.

Lord Westley stood still, watching. I knew I had little chance of avoiding being further attacked. But with my body rigid and ready, I planned to kick out at his legs with my booted foot, when I had sufficient space between us to manoeuvre myself into the right position. At that moment we were too close to each other. I must wait and take the first opportunity that presented itself and hope that I would throw off the debilitating efforts of the drug I had been given.

To my renewed horror, the knife in Westley's grip was repeatedly being slowly lowered, then raised, in front of my face, to incite fear. It did.

A sudden loud bang vibrated through the room. The dogs growled. Almost instantaneously the front door burst open. The sound cut through the lethal atmosphere. It arrested Lord Westley in his threatening lunge, disrupting the knife's passage. I twisted sideways as best I could, but the knife, still in slow flight, found a home. My injured arm began to spurt new blood. The dogs snarled menacingly but waited for a signal to attack

Wood slamming against wood reverberated throughout the house.

Two people, Mike, then Alyce, rushed in.

"NO! GO! Get out of here, NOW! " I screamed.

Vera M. Murray   Leap Year   Blood Lust

BOOK 3

THE FIRST INSTALMENT OF

ALYCE ANDERSON'S RECORD

OF THE ROCKVILLE HORROR

PUBLISHED IN QUEENSBURG'S

'TODAY'S WOMAN MAGAZINE'

CHAPTER 14

A search for the missing Greg

On February 29, 2008 I was alone with my aged Grandfather, Reverend Andrew Anderson. He lay sleeping in his hospital bed, weak, with death creeping ever closer. After Greg Allen left, my heart settled down to its normal steady pace. His sudden entrance and his presence in the room both alarmed and thrilled me.

I walked over to Grandfather to straighten his bed covers when I noticed the envelope Grandfather had wanted Greg to take with him. It was on the floor. It had either fallen off the bed, or Greg Allen had decided he had enough to take with him and dropped it. I pointed it out to Grandfather and he became very distressed. "Alyce, will you do me a great favour?" he begged.

"Of course I will. You know that."

"Please, I implore you. Take this envelope to Greg, today." Because I was frightened by his frail condition – he was on borrowed time – I would do anything to make his last days happy so I agreed. And, it would be a heaven-sent opportunity to see Greg again – this stranger who had made my heart beat faster, and disturbed my peace of mind. I had studied his features while he conversed with Grandfather. The blue eyes in his well-shaped face suited his fairness of hair and skin. I liked his lean, muscled athletic body, and knew he must play a sport of some kind. I pictured how he would look when his lips were curled in a smile and his eyes shone with mirth. I also liked his gentle tone of voice. The memory I had thus conjured up, thrilled me. I could not remember feeling that way about anyone before.

"You'll find Greg at the pub in Rockville."

I wondered how he knew. Greg had not mentioned where he was staying. I felt Grandfather was only guessing. I was convinced it could not be the hotel, unless it had been rebuilt. Either that, or it was another sign of Grandfather's state of mind. I had never been to Rockville. Grandfather insisted I would only be upset. I had never seen Grandma Ursula's grave. Although he had promised to take me there, he never did.

"I'll go tonight when my shift ends,' I told him.

"You'll have no trouble getting there. Turn into Rockville Road. It's the only one that runs off the main road between here and Little Rock. You will then come to a fork in the road. You turn right there. I'll see you when you come back for me, but you must return before midnight."

I believed him to be raving again, so I replied, to comfort him. "It'll be well before midnight. I intend to make a quick round trip."

"Perhaps . . . I'll be ready when you come for me."

I kissed his cheek before leaving to continue my rounds. I finished these as quickly as I could. I then quietly left the hospital to pick up a coat from my apartment. I would need it against the cool night air.

Once on the road in my small Ford car, I did not exceed the obligatory sixty kilometres an hour. Cars that flashed past me seemed to be driving at double that speed. The cold freaky feeling many felt when travelling along this stretch of coastal road incited them to speed.

I reached the Rockville turn-off Grandfather had described, and turned on to an overgrown track. The car bumped in and out of invisible potholes. I eventually spied the 'Welcome to Rockville' sign. Soon after I spotted the lights of the hotel. I wondered how many people lived in the town, as I had heard the quarries were closed. No one ever mentioned Rockville except in passing. It seemed to be a taboo subject.

I parked in the hotel car park, hurriedly slid out of the car, and walked inside. The clerk seemed overly pleased to see me. "You are looking for . .?"

"Greg Allen."

"Greg and Mike went into the bar. If you go down that passageway over there, you'll see the bar-room door on the right."

"Thanks." I followed his directions, but hesitated at the entrance. I could hear voices, some high, some mumbling, but something was missing. It was the laughter and high-pitched conversations usually prominent in a gathering of this kind. I slowly pushed apart the swinging doors and entered. Several customers, as well as the bar tender, noticed me, so I walked nervously up to him, feeling very much out of place.

"Looking for Greg?"

"How did you know?"

"Sixth sense lady. It's a common trait here." He gave a toothy grin. "Greg isn't here but his mate is. That's Mike Mitchell, making serious conversation with that bunch of blokes at the end of the bar."

I followed the line of his pointing finger to see an animated young man leaning on the counter. He was clinking his glass up against the man's next to him. Mike, noticing the glances in my direction from his fellow drinkers, stood upright when he saw me. He smiled the smile of a thirsty traveller who had suddenly seen an oasis in the desert.

"Are you Mike, Greg's friend?" I asked.

Mike stared unabashed, and seemed to be unable to tear his gaze away from my lips. "And who have I the pleasure of meeting?"

"I'm Alyce. Has Greg mentioned me?"

"No, the dark horse, but I see why he's kept you a secret. You could do better than him you know. I'm completely at your service." I ignored that.

"I want to see Greg. I've an important message for him from the parson."

Mike laughed. "Gone religious has he? I don't believe it, although I can see how he would be tempted if you've anything to do with a parson, respectfully said of course."

"Of course," I said absently, recalling the urgent tone of Grandfather's request. "Where can I find him? It's important. I'm in a hurry. I have to get back to Greystone."

"I think he's gone to bed. He wants to leave early in the morning. I guess he's asleep. He hasn't got the stamina I've got. I've just started my night's enjoyment. Care to join me?"

"No thank you. I'll check again. Perhaps he came in unnoticed." I turned to go.

"See you soon. The sooner the better." He made his whole attention one of admiration. "Do come back soon. I'll be waiting."

I returned to the reception area. The clerk was not present. I looked for Greg's room number. I found it written down in an open journal. I headed upstairs. On door No.13 I knocked, but there was no answer. I assumed he was asleep. I turned the handle hoping it was not locked. It swung creakily inwards. The room was empty.

About to retreat I noticed a note lying on a pillow on one of the single beds. I walked over and picked it up. It was addressed to his friend. It read. 'Mike. I've gone to the top of the mountain again, on what I hope wouldn't be a wild goose chase. If I don't return before midnight, come and get me, or, if trouble looms, get yourself out at once, and high-tail it back home.'

Why would he go to the top of the mountain at night? Had he taken Grandfather's ravings seriously? Surely not?

I returned to the lobby. The night clerk was now back on duty. I queried him about Greg's action in going up the mountain. He explained. "A simple-minded lad from this town is missing. A search party hasn't found him yet, so everyone's worried. For some reason Greg must have decided to help them look for him. That's the only reason I can think of, to make him decide to go up there tonight." The man's vision caressed the ceiling as he spoke a prayer. "God protect Joseph and Greg from the Westleys, who are cruel beyond belief."

"Joseph? You said 'Joseph.'"

"That's the boy's name . . . Joseph Allen."

Puzzled, I sank down into one of the nearby soft chairs. My mind began to oscillate between common sense and guilt. Grandfather talked as if the Joseph he sees in his nightmares is the same one now up on the mountain. But, his Joseph would be long dead, or no longer a boy. I wondered what Greg's connection was to Joseph, except that both had 'Allen' for a surname. *A relative perhaps?*

The clerk left to attend to other duties. I was alone in the lobby. I toyed with the envelope, turning, tapping my face with it; rubbing my fingers over it, wanting to open it. Grandfather had given it to me for Greg, thinking it would help protect him in some way. He had also given Greg his beloved cross and a bottle of Holy Water? *The new tablets the doctor gave him must have affected him, or perhaps those ideas are merely the ramblings of a very sick old man. No . . . that's what I thought yesterday. Now I'm completely confused. I must open the envelope.* I told myself I would be doing the correct thing, should Greg really be in danger. If there was something there to cause embarrassment, I would destroy it.

I was worried. Grandfather mentioned Greg would not be able to leave Rockville before midnight, if at all. This seemed to disturb Greg and he had shuffled his feet as if ready to run.

Then to my amazement, Grandfather had handed his cross to this stranger, who seemed reluctant to accept it. He still took it, which was even more surprising. I was not unhappy to see the end of it. It constituted a danger to him with those sharp pointed arms. His devotion to it was paramount, but he had handed it over to a complete stranger.

The next surprise was giving Greg his bottle of Holy Water. What the stranger would do with it I had no idea. Grandfather then asked me to hand him the large envelope lying on his side table. I wondered what insane thing he was going to do with it.

I did not have long to wait. Grandfather placed the envelope on the bed near Greg and said, "Take these and read them. They'll tell you everything."

I was embarrassed because I believed they held personal information. They could have no possible interest for Greg. I would not have blamed him if he had thrown everything away, the minute he was outside.

When our visitor had turned to leave, he looked into my eyes, giving me a penetrating stare. It seemed to last forever. Alarmed at my emotional reaction, I feigned interest elsewhere, grateful that Grandfather at that moment began to speak to Greg again. 'That demented lord from hell will not let you leave, but you are Joseph's only hope. You're his . . .' he had sputtered.

After marching Greg to the door I quickly moved to give him his medicine. As I was doing this the stranger left.

Time was now slipping by. I had to make a decision, now! Without further thought I ripped open the envelope and began to flick through the papers. I stopped when I found several sheets covering the history of Grandfather's early mission in the mining town of Rockville. There were events, press cuttings, and photographs of him and Grandma Ursula when he officiated in this small town. From there he catered for the spiritual needs of those living in this whole area. It included Greystone, the closest town to the north of Rockville, and Little Rock to the south and further inland.

The two looked happy and contented in these photos, but I had already seen most of them in the family albums.

The jottings though, and related photos, gave rise to a sense of urgency. I cannot explain the feeling. One photo I had not seen before was of Grandma waving goodbye to Grandfather outside this very hotel. It was the night he left for Stanholme. Later he was to return. He settled in Greystone, where I joined him. Scrolled across the photo was, 'She stayed behind to get things ready for the new pastor. She died that night.' The sorrow was palpable. He blamed himself for having left her behind.

It haunted him. It affected his mind and caused him to be confined, on and off, to different mental institutions.

Another photo I had not seen before showed each of them with an arm around a thin boy with Down-Syndrome features. I decided he must be about twelve years of age. He somehow reminded me of Greg, yet I could not think in what way.

There was one of a Lord Flurice Henry Argyle Westley with Lady Phoebe. They were dressed in expensive designer-made clothes. Their faces; his white and handsome; hers beautiful, were cold as if chiselled from ivory. Both possessed piercing dark eyes. Their narrow lips expressed ill-disguised smirks, which caused me to shudder at the shallowness and coldness revealed.

I skimmed quickly over the faded writing on several pages to come to one with the heading, 'The Evil One's Marked Victims'. They all carried an almost identical star-shaped birthmark. I did not know what it all meant, but every surname was the same. It was 'Allen.' Then I recalled Grandfather examining Greg's wrist, and I did catch a glance of red smudged lines before he dropped his arm.

While continuing to run my eyes down the page I stopped in amazement. The last name on the list of 'Marked Victims' was 'Gregory (Greg) Allen'. It was the only name without a line drawn through it. The previous name, Thomas (Tom) Allen rang a bell. The common belief was that Tom Allen was a murder victim. All details were in the local newspapers. *Is Greg to be the next so-called marked victim? That's what Grandfather must have been thinking when he made the list.*

As I flicked through more pages, one picture stood out. It showed a graveyard with a pencilled note that read 'Rockville Cemetery'. I could not recognise the background, for it sat in the midst of almost completely desolate ground, with nothing around or beyond it but piles of old timber, and a solitary shed.

A further photo included rows of graves. In the foreground there were four, already dug, but empty, although tombstones had been put in place with each one. They were old and the inscriptions on them were barely visible, but squinting, I read 'Ursula Anderson', my Grandmother's name, on the one adjoining the four empty ones,

Turning the photo over I found Grandfather's handwriting on the back. 'I can't join you my dear until the evil ones are despatched to Hell. I have to stay until I can help rid the town of their leap year blood lust and bring peace to all. Please forgive me, but one day I will claim my grave site next to yours.'

I tried to fathom the mystery of the other empty graves, open, waiting. Were they for Greg, Mike and myself, the only strangers in town? Surely not, as they looked as if they had been dug a long time ago. Grandfather had told me Rockville was caught in a time warp. But Grandfather was not coherent, or was he? Four empty grave sites, lying next to Grandma Ursula's but still empty . . . created in readiness for four people, but who are they?

There was also a statement declaring that Lord Westley was responsible for all the Allen deaths. *If, as Grandfather claims, that the Westleys return from the grave, why didn't Grandfather find someone who could deal with this type of phenomenon . . . get help? Perhaps he'd tried.*

The last page read, 'Joseph comes to me, begging for help to return the Westleys to hell and free the town and its people, so they can finally be at rest.

Joseph told me what happened on the day I left. He said he had stolen dynamite from the quarry. He set it off one night, to get rid of Westley's sheds. They had been placed on what he considered was his beach.

These are his words as I recall them. 'I climbed along the rocks 'til I got close to my cave further along the beach. I took the detonation cords as far as they'd go. I lit them with the blasting caps I stole, like they did at the quarry. I climbed to the top of the rock wall to watch.

Then came this big bang. I was glad I took the earmuffs with me. The huts and the cliff started shivering and falling down like at the quarry. The cliff house was going back and forth, like jelly. Someone was yelling. Rocks and dirt came down like rain. The Manor House started falling over. I knew the Westleys were inside. Rocks were jumping at me. I was slipping. I tried to hold on to boulders but my hands kept slipping off. Then the jumping water sucked me in. I was happy 'cos tomorrow the beach would be mine.

But the Westleys keep coming back on the same date every leap year to take revenge. I come back, to try to stop them. Help me Pastor Anderson. I don't want any more Allens to die, because of what I did.'

I was shocked at Grandfather's tale. I offered up a prayer for help. It came. I remained calm, at least outwardly. I considered this revelation in the same light as a death-cheating operation, such as I have witnessed in the hospital's operating theatre. On the bottom of the last sheet Grandfather had written 'What seemed both true and tragic can be a mistaken belief, and the truth something very different . . . as Joseph and I both know.' *Perhaps this is an expression of Grandfather's guilt at leaving Grandma on the day she died.*

My body slowly relaxed. I was again in control. I shoved everything back into the envelope. Greg was in danger. I had to find him, warn him. The deaths were all connected with the Westleys and their Manor House. *Greg's in that area right now. Does his name on Grandfather's list mean his death is imminent? Perhaps he's to be the first to fill one of those empty graves. I must warn him.*

I needed his friend Mike to help me find Greg. Despite the need for speed, I did not run. I did not want to draw unwelcome attention to myself, or invite unwanted questioning.

Little interest was taken when I re-entered the bar. I asked the barman where Mike was. He pointed to a table where Mike was seated with three others. He was deep in conversation.

I walked over and touched his arm to get his attention. "Mike, I want to talk to you, privately."

Mike gave a grin and a wink to his friends as he rose. He followed me, saying, "It'll be a pleasure." He led me to a table in the far corner. We sat close. I made sure no one else could hear what I was about to say.

"Greg's in grave danger. I want you to come with me to find him."

"You must be suffering from delusions. He's gone to bed, or he's out enjoying himself. Forget Greg, I'll go anywhere else with you. Just name it, pretty lady."

"I'm serious Mike. He's gone up the mountain. He's in danger." He showed surprise as he realised that I was deadly serious.

"What? I can't believe he'd go up there again. I don't know what's possessed him, but he's been acting strange ever since he returned from his trek this morning. He seems to have developed a persecution complex. He wanted to get out of Rockville as quickly as possible.

Anyway, the locals are getting together a search party for a lost kid. Although it's late, it seems the boy's somehow impaired, and could get disorientated. They're now focusing on searching the mountaintop. If up there he could fall from the cliff into the sea. Apparently the sea fascinates him. So what would make Greg go up there again? I know. He said he left some beer and sandwiches behind this morning. Maybe he went to retrieve them."

"Mike, this is no time for jokes. We have to find him. Please Mike, come with me"

"Just wait." Mike pulled out his mobile phone. He dialled Greg's number, and then put it to his ear. He jerked it quickly away. "There's only loud shrieks coming through. It's eerie. It must be something in the atmosphere." He dropped the phone back into his shirt pocket.

"Are you sure he's gone up there. It's the last place I'd want to be. They mutter on here about a demon from hell, a voice on the wind, and other weird happenings. How did you find out he's gone there?"

"He left a note." I handed it to him. I hoped he would not ask where I had found it so I merely told him. "It was left for you. It was the hotel clerk who said that Greg might have gone to help find that confused child, because he was up there earlier and may have caught a glimpse of him and would know where to look."

"I'll have to admit, that'd be Greg, always preparing for his next newspaper article. I don't take the note seriously. Greg is very melodramatic."

I took out the photos of the graves. I handed them to him. "Please look at these. Four are empty, waiting." He took them, holding them close to his face in order to see properly in the subdued lighting. I wanted to show Mike the rest of the photos, and the other newspaper clippings, but time was running out. Greg was already in some kind of danger. I felt certain of it.

"I can't read any names on them and they look ancient. Something left over from Halloween is it?" He smiled an even smile.

Becoming impatient, I thrust the Allen list of names in front of him. "The heading is 'All have the Mark of the Victim'. Greg's name's on it, and the man listed above Greg's is commonly believed to have been murdered here in Rockville. I assume the others were all murdered here too. All had the Allen surname, like Greg. I believe it says enough to warrant finding out if Greg's okay."

Mike twisted his mouth and muttered, "Umm, interesting, but can't it wait? He may have gone up there with other searchers. Who knows? He might walk in any moment."

I could not stop the hot blood rush up my neck to colour my cheeks. "You're evading the issue. They've told you the same story I read in Grandfather's papers. There's an evil lord, a demon from hell up there, and you're running scared."

Mike looked at me steadily. "I'll make you a deal. If we go up the mountain to rescue him, and I'm right. He's enjoying himself with some chick in the Manor House they talk about, you must persuade Greg to return the hundred dollars he won from me." He grinned. "I'll enjoy seeing his face when we intrude on his night out, or . . ." He stopped speaking for a moment, smiled roguishly, then continued. "Perhaps this is your way to get a male all to yourself in a deserted spot? If so, I think it should become the fashion all over the country."

I was angry. My face was burning like a beacon. I knew it would be bright red, but showing impatience would not help. I could see that even in his fog of grog he was beginning to listen. "I can't speak for Greg, but if you're right and he doesn't give you the money back, I'll give it to you myself. We have to go. Somehow my Grandfather knew Greg would return to the mountain tonight. He knew there was danger, so he gave Greg . . . how shall I put it . . . some protection."

"Ah . . . Greg's seen a parson. Is marriage in mind?"

I ignored that. When Mike still did not move, I stood and picked up his jacket. I handed it to him, to force him to hurry. "Please come quickly. Your friend's in danger. I know it. If you don't, I'll go by myself."

"I could never refuse a request from a beautiful girl." Mike moved, although slowly, from his chair, and took his jacket from me. He glanced around the room and directed his attention to those close by. "Anyone else like to come up the mountain with us?" No one moved. "They must all be scared of the Voice on the Wind, or the lord who brings death with him."

We left the hotel. Mike sounded dismayed as he glanced back. "No one's joining us. Maybe they're not keen on searching for the boy at night. Of course they could be planning to search the top of the cliffs, but not just yet. They may be waiting for the results of other searches made around town, before making a perilous climb up the mountain at night"

I said nothing. It was obvious Mike wanted other companions, not this strange girl who did not seem to speak sense to him. If I had asked him to keep me company at the hotel, I'm sure he would have jumped at the offer.

"You must be an optimist Mike. I didn't expect anyone."

"I was hoping, but more than two's a crowd they say. I hope Greg appreciates my interest in his welfare when I take back that hundred dollars." He laughed a happy laugh as he visualised Greg's reaction.

I was overwhelmed by a creeping feeling of dread. I kept thinking of what I had been reading. Although the photographs were not recent, if Grandfather's grave was waiting, ready for him next to Grandma Ursula's, the other future occupants of the three remaining empty ones may also be still alive. They may even be us.

As we walked, the puzzle still consumed me. It was likely that Grandfather's Joseph, and the Joseph on the mountain must be connected, perhaps through family ties. If not, it could be the same person. To Grandfather there existed a time warp. I tried to link up all the different snippets of information. It was Grandfather's belief that a serial murderer, in the shape of an evil spectre from hell, returned to Rockville as Lord Westley, seeking revenge, so perhaps Joseph could come back also. If this were true, could we change the course of events, or was it already ordained? I was appalled by that prospect.

Mike and I found the steps easily enough, but the climb ahead was steep in parts and rough. Fortunately I was wearing my low-heeled, rubber-soled work shoes.

Mike produced a torch. In my impatience to get to Greg it did not occur to me that I might need one.

"This is Greg's. I borrowed it. Mine's too big to fit in my pocket." He had a sheepish tone to his voice. "I was expecting to invite a young lady for a walk along the beach tonight, so decided I could need some light."

It had a weak beam but it chased away the closer shadows. It did little to clearly show up the true depth and unevenness of the stone steps and the length of the winding path we travelled on our way up the cliff face.

On reaching the top, we paused for breath before proceeding to push aside greenery that blocked our path. This revealed a double iron gate, with an almost lace-like design in wrought iron strips across both sides. After reading the name on it we walked through, to be stunned by the sudden appearance before us, of a lovely Manor House.

Before we had the opportunity to absorb the sight of the magnificent scene of the Mansion nestled in a large ornate garden, loud voices were escaping through the open windows. This grated on our eardrums. Angry voices, blood-chilling laughter, followed by a scream, caused me to freeze in my tracks. The scream was from a young voice. Joseph came instantly to mind. Mike ran, and I followed him along the path leading to the front entrance. Mike immediately threw his body against the door the instant we reached it. It burst open and crashed back against the wall behind it. I was close on his heels as we raced in.

No one was in the outer room. We kept running towards an archway, from which emanated the sound of blood-curdling laughter and a dog's growl.

At the entrance to a bar-library we stopped abruptly at what we saw. My stomach turned in sickening circles.

Greg was tied to a chair. A woman, Lady Westley from the photo I had seen, was on one side of him. A large dog, a Rottweiler, hemmed him in on the other. Another large dog was crouched down, close to the Rottweiler. A man with the most evil face I have ever seen – the man in Grandfather's photo, Lord Westley – was leaning over Greg. This demonic man was holding a blood-dripping knife over Greg's face. Blood was on Greg's jacket, along his shoulder and down his sleeve

I stepped back, horrified. I choked, dragging my eyes away to stare at a young boy. The youngster's face was ashen. His eyes bulged. A small chubby hand with short fingers covered his mouth. *Joseph?* He looked to be the child in that photo. *Is he a resurrection from the dead, as Grandfather believed?* That thought drifted briefly across my mind and vanished as the boy put out his hand. I noticed a birthmark on his neck. Was that what Grandfather called 'The Mark of the Victim'? He had said the same thing when looking at Greg's wrist. Revelation was instant. Grandfather was never demented. He was on a mission.

I hurried over and put my arm around Joseph. We clung together as we watched the knife being raised high over Greg's face. Joseph buried his face in my shoulder. I wanted to shut my eyes but they refused to close.

Greg stared at us; momentarily disbelieving we were actually present. Quickly recovering he screamed, "Get out of here. Get the hell out. NOW."

BOOK 4

THE EVIL LORD LAUGHS,

INTENT ON DEALING OUT DEATH

TO THE MARKED ONE,

AND ALL WHO INTERFERE

CHAPTER 15

Greg and Mike's fight the devious evil ones.

I HEARD Mike's voice calling my name. It followed the loud bang of the front door being flung open. *Good loyal Mike.*

"Greg, for God's sake, are you in here?" He was yelling. When he became visible I shouted back, "Get out of here. Get the hell out . . . NOW!" With a twist in the guts I saw Alyce was with him.

They stopped in the archway, rooted to the spot in horror as they faced a scene of bloody chaos. They seemed unable to move, as if hypnotized. "Get out now!" I shouted again.

All planned movement by the Westleys was halted at Mike and Alyce's sudden noisy entrance. Their appearance had put my assailants off guard. Surprise had interrupted their 'happy hour'. Westley still held the dagger suspended several centimetres above my face but he had relaxed the tightness of his grip. This lasted but a few moments before the smirk returned to Westley's face. He showed pleasure at the unexpected increase in his audience.

Lady Phoebe stared at Mike and Alyce, before stepping protectively towards her husband. This caused her to slacken her hold on the rope still twisted around the chair and me. The rope ends slipped from her hands as she moved forward, and away from me.

I had to get free and act quickly if we were to survive. I strained hard against the confines of the rope. It loosened further. Rustus snarled menacingly and saliva dripped from its jowls whenever I moved. It came closer. Its panting breath was warm on my neck. Queenie moved to settle down closer, waiting behind Rustus. I shuddered, expecting teeth to bite into my flesh, but Rustus drew back a little and became motionless, waiting. The now slack rope was loose enough to give me some free movement, but I stayed rigid. I had to think. I had to get my poorly functioning brain into gear, and quickly.

With my only 'weapon', my clenched fists, I was ready when given the opportunity, to bury them in Westley's face. Having shrugged off the presence of the intruders, Westley turned his attention back to me. His eyes bored into mine. They were hooded slits that revealed fathomless gloomy pits like the eyes of a viper when ready to strike.

In a sudden movement Westley raised the blade, already smeared with my blood. He held it there. I twisted my neck sideways in any effort to avert my face, expecting him to strike, but Westley still held back, sneering. No doubt he was trying to increase our terror. Beads of sweat formed on my face and body. The effect of the drug that had numbed my brain was beginning to dissipate. A feeling of desperation rose. While Westley was concentrating on playing his horror game on me, and ignoring the intruders, Mike crouched in attack position. He waited.

"Flurice, look out for the new one!" Phoebe was alert as ever.

Westley turned his attention back on Mike, still waiting for the right moment but poised ready. This gave me the opportunity to make my move. Discarding the loose rope, I cast it aside. With all the speed I could muster I jumped to my feet, immediately flinging myself away from any immediate grasps from Phoebe or the dogs. At the same time I was aiming my fist towards the side of Westley's head. The blow landed, but he did not falter. A fly would have got more attention. His hand holding the knife did drop a little, but was slowly raised again. I quickly took a step back. The back of my legs contacted the edge of chair. I became unbalanced, and my body collapsed back into it.

Rustus had been cowed by my unexpected move. It did not attack. The other dog, Queenie, grumbled low in its throat, also waiting for a command, but the Westley's gaze was now trained on an anxious Mike.
"My dear Phoebe, do control that skittish Allen fellow while I deal with this new irritant."

Phoebe did not look at me. "Rustus, on guard," she commanded. Rustus again sank down into an attacking mode. He growled deeply and bared his teeth. I did not fear any deadly attack from Rustus. Death was the providence of the Westleys, not their dogs.

I edged forward to rise quickly and strike Westley from the rear as he turned back in Mike's direction. Rustus barked twice as I moved, and a deep warning snarl came from the throat of Queenie. "Hold him Rustus!" Phoebe had barely turned her head. Alarmed as the dog sprang at my throat, I quickly raised my left arm to protect my face. Not daunted, Rustus buried his teeth into the thick leather of my jacket sleeve. Its jaws locked. Queenie snarled. I steeled myself for a new bout of pain as I tugged vigorously to free myself, but the teeth remained clamped together. It was impossible to move away without inviting further attack. The dog stayed quiet, and motionless, while staring at me with unblinking eyes, while Queenie rose and held herself in readiness to join in, should an attack be ordered. *If I could only discard my jacket I might have a chance.* I carefully and slowly began undoing the buttons with my free hand. The dogs watched every move I made.

Westley turned his head slightly towards Phoebe. Mike's opportunity had come, however slight. With clawed fingers in a classic football tackle, he propelled himself forward. Westley swung completely around to thwart Mike's attack. His body was bent, his head lowered. He was poised like the fabled devil cats of ancient legends, ready and deadly.

Mike's outstretched hands contacted Westley's shoulders with extreme force. Unable to stop, his head met Westley's with a loud hollow sound. Mike reeled, stunned. He tottered on the edge of unconsciousness though still on his feet. Westley blinked but remained unaffected. The sound of combined crying and smothered screaming came from Alyce and Joseph.

Phoebe moved closer to Mike. She encircled Mike's throat with her arm, pulling his head back. Mike was too dazed to resist. Westley smiled at his wife. "Thanks dearest. You're a great help."

"I learnt it from you, dear one, and practice makes perfect, even though it's on a substitute Allen."

"I most certainly agree," Westley spoke as he levelled the point of the knife directly towards Mike's eye. Mike's head fell back as blood spurted from Mike's face. It flowed like a stream down his cheek. "You filthy swine!" I yelled.

"My turn dear one. You can't have all the fun," spoke she-devil Phoebe as they both released their grip on Mike. He fell to the floor unconscious.

"Of course my darling."

"You filthy rotten swine!" I kept shouting.

Unconcerned by my outbursts, Lady Phoebe crouched down to rip Mike's shirt open. Buttons popped and settled on the carpet. One pinged against the bar. Her long sharp fingernails traced lines across his stomach in the rough shape of a star. She followed this with the point of a knife drawn from some hidden pocket in her dress. Blood oozed and spread, covering the whiteness of his skin with a sickly coating of slow, seeping, life-blood. I was ill with horror and dread.

Westley, smiling with obvious delight, reached over and stroked his wife's arm several times. They did not glance back at me. They were enjoying the spectacle of Mike, collapsed, bloody, and comatose, stretched out on the floor.

I was more desperate than ever to rid myself of my jacket, still cemented in the jaws of the dog. I squirmed as I tried to get my other arm out of its sleeve. I scraped that section against the back of the chair to pull it down on that side. I succeeded, and the now free part of the jacket fell down behind my back. The arm was now free. Rustus curled his lips in a fang-baring display of displeasure, so I worked even slower. I now had to get the other arm out. Twisting my body I gently wriggled my imprisoned arm upwards, until it too was jerked free. This forced Rustus, still with clamped teeth, to fall back, taking the jacket with him. I quickly cast it over the heads of both dogs. Rustus began to vigorously shake it, while Queenie, making short sharp barks, began to wriggle her way from under it. I had room to manoeuvre at last. I stood up.

The Westleys' attention reverted back to me, drawn by the sounds made by the dogs. They both stared at my stomach region. *The cross! I had forgotten the cross.* With no jacket covering it, it was now exposed. Westley, expressionless, sucked in his breath. Phoebe showed veiled concern. *Why? They still have the upper hand in this skirmish. Is she planning her next move to be on my stomach?*

"The cross . . . use the cross!" screamed a voice. It was Alyce's.

Of course, the cross! I pulled it out. *What am I supposed to do with it? Do I wave it in front of Westley's face . . . put it like a shield between us . . . make a cross over him . . . pray perhaps?* These questions came in a torrent, chasing each other in my desperate search for a quick answer. It came. With its sharp points the cross was like a dagger. I raised it ready to strike.

"You think that will save you?" Phoebe laughed flatly.

Westley became possessed. He flung himself at me. His casual, confident, attitude had vanished. Knife aloft, he forced me to retreat. I scuttled away from the chair, but found myself backed up against the bar, with Westley closing in. He made one wide swipe at me with the knife. I ducked sideways and fended him off with my outstretched arm, which caught him near his shoulder, propelling him sideways. In the process his elbow swung and cracked against my arm. The cross was knocked out of my grip. It flew out of my control. One sharp-pointed side arm entered the soft pile of the carpet, while the opposite arm pointed directly upwards towards the ceiling.

As Westley tried to recover, I swung my foot, kicking his legs from under him. He sagged and began to crumble. He twisted his body in an effort to regain his balance, but fell, face downward, on to the rapier point of the cross' arm. It buried itself between his ribs. Westley convulsed for a few seconds, then rolled on to his back, taking the imbedded cross with him. His fingers grasped at air and his eyes stared with surprise, as he gulped in air.

Phoebe, who had been watching, now let out a loud piercing cry. With mind-numbing wordless wails she flung herself upon her husband's jerking body. Immediately the razor sharp point protruding skyward from Westley's chest punctured her soft skin and entered her heart. Her scream shattered my nerves completely. In a last desperate manoeuvre, as her life slowly ebbed away, she turned his face to hers and their lips were joined in a final kiss, uniting their bodies and their loyalty to each other. They fell limp together. The dogs crawled to their master's side, nuzzled Flurice's outstretched hand and whimpered.

I had witnessed their demise with nausea, morbid fascination, and relief; all jumbled up inside me.

"The Holy Water . . . use the Holy Water." Alyce shouted at me from where she now knelt beside the stricken Mike. I groped inside my shirt pocket. I was past wondering if it worked. *It they're already dead what difference will it make?* I popped out the cork. *Now what do I do with it?*

"Sprinkle it over them." Alyce must have noticed my hesitation. She chanted words I could not comprehend. Are *they prayers? Well, we badly need them.*

I stood over the bodies of the Westleys until almost all the contents had been sprinkled over the Westleys. I then scattered the last few drops over the dogs. Loud hissing sounds followed as if water had dropped on a hot stovetop. Steam arose into the air from the bodies of the Westleys and their dogs. *Has the Holy Water dissolved them all? Have they returned to the depths of hell?* I did not know. All I knew was that the Westleys and their dogs were gone.

I ran to where Mike was lying unconscious on the floor. One eye was covered in blood and more oozed from his cuts. "Mike! Mike! For God's sake hang in there."

"He'll die if we don't get him to the hospital quickly." Alyce spoke as she used Mike's shirt to stem the flow of blood.

Thank God she's a nurse.

Joseph hurried over. He briefly embraced me. "Thanks nephew," he said as he clasped my hot hand in his cold one. *Now I'm his nephew. What next?* But, as he released my hand I saw on his neck a birthmark identical in shape to mine. I did not know what to believe any more. *Is Joseph a ghost too? No, he can't be. He's just a simple boy wanting to help rid the town of its haunting horror.* I stubbornly refused to let go of my disbelief, that the dead had any power or influence over the living, least of all, actually returning from the grave. *Surely reality is the only truth there is, not some conjuring trick?* I tried hard to believe it was some trick, but I could not.

Joseph tugged at my sleeve to get my full attention. "After you get Mike to the hospital it'll be close to midnight. Then you must go to the cove and find my cave. Go through the park. There's a big tree. You'll find it at the back. After that, you have to get the parson 'cos he'll know what to do."

I was about to say, 'No thanks, enough's enough,' but Alyce stopped me by pressing her hand on my arm. "We will Joseph," she said as she squeezed my wrist before dropping it. "Don't worry. God's peace'll be with you soon."

With Alyce's help I straddled Mike across my shoulders for the trudge back down the mountain.

Joseph slipped from the Manor and was nowhere to be seen.

Alyce and I were clumsy in our lop-sided trip down. Alyce kept up with me and held Mike's head steady. Mike seemed to grow heavier by the minute. My head pounded. My injured arm ached madly. I stumbled several times. This forced us to stop to catch our breath and readjust ourselves. I could feel fresh blood spreading over my body from the exertion. It was Mike's blood mingling with mine. Reaching the top of the final set of steps I tripped on the root of a tree across the path and almost fell. I began to plunge forward, but regained my balance, but not before the sharp points of broken branches scratched our faces. Mike's head came in contact with a heavier offshoot. After standing for several minutes to recover, we continued on. I began to doubt that Mike would survive.

It's lucky Alyce has her car here and we don't have to rely on my bike. "You'll have to bring me back for our bikes," I told Alyce. "They're still parked near the hotel."

Alyce sighed. 'Yes Greg, but they're safe. No one's going to steal them, wherever they are."

We finally reached the car. I propped the unconscious Mike up on the back seat. "Greg, while you're driving I'll keep an eye on Mike," Alyce said.

"Right . . . you're the nurse," I muttered. I was operating like a wooden puppet, worried sick not knowing if Mike would make it.

Alyce climbed in beside Mike and placed his head against her shoulder.

The drive to the hospital seemed endless. When we reached the entrance, Alyce told me to turn off the headlights. I did, not questioning why. I rolled the car close to the front door. I braked, causing loose gravel to crunch and shoot out from under the wheels. We waited; concerned that someone might see us. We saw no one.

Alyce helped me lift Mike out of the car. I clutched him to me. One bloody cheek rested against my shoulder. I was ready to run inside and shout for help, thus saving precious seconds, but Alyce was standing in the way. "Wait Greg. I'll see if anyone's there. If there is, we'll have to wait."

"He can't wait. He could die." I could not bring myself to look closely at him.

"No one must see us. There'd be too many questions we can't answer. We also have to get Grandfather without anyone seeing us."

I was exhausted. I wanted to say, 'Not the parson. Leave him where he is. I've had enough,' but I could not.

Alyce peered through the glass front door. She beckoned me. I responded quickly and together we lay Mike on a stretcher inside. Alyce, with her finger now poised over a red emergency buzzer said, "I'll keep pressing the button until I hear footsteps. You go to the car. Be ready to leave the minute I come out."

I ran to the car and climbed in, to find the motor still running. A few seconds later Alyce flung herself through the open front passenger door, slamming it behind her. "Park as close as you can to the back door. Grandfather can't walk far."

The last thing I needed now, was anything more to do with Rockville or the parson. I did not want to be involved in anything Joseph had raved on about, especially this cave in the cove. Mike was as safe as he could be. I refused to imagine Mike not recovering. I wanted to say 'forget your Grandfather. He's safe,' until I looked into the begging eyes in Alyce's face. I do not know why, but I swallowed the words. I swung the car around and drew it to a stop at the door that allowed a quick entrance to the parson's room.

On entering his room with Alyce, I was speechless. Where was the dried up, dying man of earlier today? He looked so much stronger, and was sitting on the side of his bed, dressed in a priest's robes. He held a prayer book in one hand. "I knew you'd come for me," he said as he slid off the bed. He walked towards us at a quick shuffle. I would not have believed this possible after seeing him earlier.

What are we supposed to do with him at Rockville? Alyce seemed to know. She kept asking him if he was feeling strong enough to go with us. "Of course I am. God has restored my strength to carry out what has to be done now." He spoke without any sign of his previous shortage of breath.

As he was receiving all the assistance he needed from Alyce, I hurried back to the car. I had the doors open in readiness, but Alyce closed the front passenger door. "I'll get in the back with Grandfather. He may need me." Alyce helped him to stoop low to climb in, and settled herself beside him.

I drove the Ford out of the hospital grounds with the car lights turned off. A police car passed us, entering. I took no notice, but Alyce uttered, "Drive faster Greg. It's the police. They've seen us."

It's the police who should be handling this. But I kept driving at a speed that rattled every part of the old car, threatening it with internal collapse at any moment. We were feeling pleased that we had come as far as we had without discovery, when we heard a police siren blasting away. Although still some distance away it was heading in our direction. With their speed it would not be long before they flagged us down.

Suddenly we were bulleting towards the back of a lumbering shape. It was a loaded semi-trailer chugging along. I had no chance of stopping in time to avoid barging into it, but I had to try. I swung the wheel. The Ford swayed dangerously with the sudden change in its course, but steadied itself fairly quickly on the wrong side of the road. The semi-trailer slowed as I swung back to be in the lead. This shut off our view of the police car and their sighting of us.

We rounded a sharp curve in the road. Both the semi-trailer and police car were still lost from sight. I slowed down slightly before skidding into Rockville Road. The trees would shade us from the view from the main road. We heard the police car siren rising and falling as it passed the turnoff. It was heading towards Little Rock. We were now free of them, at least for the moment. I turned on the car's headlights.

In Rockville's main street the hotel's lights were still glowing. "Stop over on that grass near the park, Greg. It should be the closest spot to start looking for that cave Joseph told us about."

This was no time for me to wonder why Alyce was so determined to do what Joseph wanted us to do. I knew that she was going to continue with this madness. I felt I had no choice but to follow her. *What's so important about Joseph's cave?*

"I'll get some of the locals to help us," was my first offer.

"You don't understand. We have to do this ourselves. The police will be here eventually, and it's close to midnight. We must do as Joseph says – be at the cave just after midnight." *If we do get there at Joseph's designated time do we get a prize? Ha. Ha!*

Alyce opened the glove box and brought out a large torch, precious now in this situation. It had become tar black away from the glow from the hotel and the few streetlights. "This torch is must stronger than yours. Anyway, yours is still on the mountain somewhere."

The parson's voice came from inside the car. "I'll wait until you return. That's when I'll be needed."

"We won't be long." Alyce assured her Grandfather. *I hope she's right.*

I began to follow the hurrying Alyce through the park, much against my better judgement. *One of my grandmother's sayings was, 'in for a penny, in for a pound.' What made me think of that now?* I plunged into the surrounding darkness behind Alyce, who began slicing it apart with the torch rays. At the edge of the winding path Alyce paused. *Why is she delaying?* When I reached her she put a hand on my arm. "The ground's shaking. It's midnight. Can't you feel it?"

"No."

"Come on Greg, we have work to do, and quickly, before the time warp starts operating forward again."

"What?"

"Later . . . come on. We have to hurry, before everything returns to normal."

CHAPTER 16

Alyce and Greg search for the mysterious cave.

As a stole of blackness draped itself around me I grimly wondered what lay ahead. The cave could be filled with water if the tide was high. *Will Alyce still want to go in? That wouldn't surprise me.*

"You are coming aren't you Greg?" I blinked in the sudden glare as Alyce brandished the light of the torch over me. I realised I had made no effort to reach her side.

"I was just thinking."

Alyce quickened her step when I caught up with her. At the end of the park she probed the bushes with the illumination of the torchlight until she perceived a gap in a tangle of leaves and twigs. "This must be the way." She sounded more pleased than seemed warranted.

We pushed the wayward growth widely apart for us to pass through. On either side shadows loomed up and around. They scurried into hollow places when the torch shone in their particular direction. We were now forced to traverse hard ground, dried grass, and gravel. We reached a low breakwater that I assumed had been built to block any crashing waves from entering the hotel grounds during king tides.

In silence we proceeded to jump over, and sidestep, boulders, which increased in size as we moved towards the cave area. My legs felt like pulped grain. The exertion caused my wounds to ooze blood. I wanted to sit down and not bother getting up again, but Alyce was relying on me. In turn, I trusted her instincts. I did not think she would be following this through without good reason.

We reached a wall of rocks in the cove, which Westley could have intended to use as a foundation for the beach house he planned to build. By sight and feel we found a gap sufficiently wide for us to climb through. We did this carefully, fearful that a loose rock might break free.

Once on the other side, we gingerly felt our way along the base of the barrier. We tried to keep our balance on smaller rocks before being forced to step into yielding mud combined with sand in this eerie cove. Alyce remarked, "I'm glad it's not high tide. This stinking mud's made the rocks slippery. Joseph didn't tell us about this. From what he had said earlier, I expected to find his sandy beach . . . whoops!" Alyce began to topple. Quickly I grabbed her coat and pulled her upright.

"Give me the torch Alyce. With all this moss and seagrass it's hard to know where to step. I'll go first. I've no idea where we're heading so you'll have to direct me. Hang on to my shirt for support. It'll be easier on my arm."

"Sorry Greg, I forgot."

"The arm's not too bad. I was lucky, not like Mike."

"I'm so worried about him. It's my fault he was there."

"Your fault?"

Between deep breaths she said, "I'll tell you later. I need all my breath now to keep wading through all this muck."

"The way you keep going amazes me." *She's a gem. Nothing seems to faze her. She's acting as if she were on a crusade.*

We carefully changed places. I could now test each foothold with my weight before Alyce stepped into the footprint I made. I did not wish either of us to fall into some deep invisible mud-filled hole and be sucked under in this God-forgotten place. We painstakingly continued – our clammy wet boots a hindrance. We kept wading for what seemed an age, plodding through the shallow, sucking water of the outgoing tide. It filled our shoes with both water and mud. I thought nothing more could possibly irritate me. I was wrong.

"Shine the light higher Greg. I think that's Joseph's tree over on that higher section." We soon reached our first objective. The tree was old, judging from its rough thick trunk. Saplings had shot out from its base, forming a green barrier. While seeking a secure footing we almost tripped over exposed roots twisted like aged rheumatic fingers. No cave was visible, and no indentations showed on either side of the trunk to suggest one. But, if Joseph was right, it was there somewhere.

I joined Alyce in breaking off branches that snapped easily. We were forced to pull apart tall saplings and weeds whose tops were above the mud. We went on clearing away the debris around and behind it, to finally expose a repulsive dark orifice. Although hidden behind the trees, the entrance was wide enough and high enough to allow us to enter.

On entering I walked slowly, shining the torch over the ground, searching for any sign of snakes or other deadly creatures. As I swirled it around I do not know what I expected, but it was not what I saw in sudden horror. Three human bodies lay against the far wall. Their open glassy eyes reflected the torchlight. I quickly diverted the light towards the ground. "They can't be bodies Alyce, can they?"

Alyce did not answer but looked at me and sighed. Joseph and the parson's incredulous outbursts had made little sense to me. My chief interest had been to leave Rockville as far behind as possible. If Mike had not been so stubborn I would not have been in this situation, although, if it had to happen, Alyce would have been my choice of a companion.

Alyce squeezed my hand. "Let's get it over with. We have to hurry. The bodies won't stay like they are now for too long. The change is coming."

"Okay," I muttered, not knowing what she meant.

We bent lower and moved, to stand inside the cave proper. Alyce took the torch from my numb fingers and illuminated the strangely intact faces of the dead. The light created grotesque shadows on the corpses – a woman, a man and a young boy. *It can't be Lord and Lady Westley, and Joseph. We left them in the Manor House. Joseph was alive. Now he's dead too.* "How did they get here?" I looked at Alyce for any answer.

"Don't be surprised Greg. There was a time warp, as Grandfather always claimed. We are back in the Rockville of 1988. After the explosion the bodies were sucked in here by the wash caused when the cliff face fell. We have to do what should have been done all those years ago. That is, keep the Westleys in hell, and Joseph in heaven." Alyce had succeeded in snapping me out of the paralysing funk I was in, but no glimmer of understanding filtered through to my brain. *1988, but surely that's a joke? Has a demented old man sucked us both in, or only his granddaughter?*

"Greg, hurry up. I feel sick too, but there's no one else to do it. We must get them out of here for burial. That's what Joseph and Grandfather want . . . to bring the whole ghastly chapter to a close. That's what we're here for."

I forced myself out of my inertia. "How are we supposed to do that?"

"Whatever way we can. Drag them if we have to. Grandfather will be at the cemetery waiting."

"Cemetery? I didn't know there was one. Shouldn't we go back to the hotel and ring the police? They could handle this better than us." My question went unanswered. I wondered again why Mike and I had not noticed the graveyard before.

"Let's take Joseph out first. He'll have more time with Grandfather."

Take them out . . . us? I didn't think Alyce meant what she said earlier. This ordeal's definitely affecting her. I shivered with cold horror at the thought.

Alyce made the first move towards the bodies. Facing Westley, she pulled out the cross protruding from his chest. I flinched as I moved to reluctantly take over the gruesome task that lay ahead. Their faces and arms bore burn marks, but the bodies were strangely warm, though their clothes were wet and filthy. They were dressed exactly as I had seen them earlier. *Was it earlier? It's too confusing. I'll think about it later.*

Joseph was light and easy to carry. His face wore a smile of contentment as I scooped him up in the arms. The return trip was quicker. We retraced our steps by inserting each foot into a previous print. We found the park, still in light fog. Once through it, Alyce began to swing the torch to left and right, until we located the Ford.

"There's Grandfather." There was relief in Alyce's voice. The parson's upright figure stood facing rows of graves. *The cemetery . . . so close?* We proceeded to lay

Joseph at the parson's feet. He bent and touched the boy's cheek. Silently we left them together, relieved that the fog had not yet covered the whole area.

I decided to tackle Lord Westley next, and leave Phoebe to last. As expected we made the slowest pace with Lord Westley. He was heavier than expected. I turned my eyes away from the smirk on his face and the staring eyes. They seemed to be still alive. My arms were beginning to feel disconnected from me. I had to lower the body to the ground on several occasions in order to regain energy. We were forced at times, to drag the body over soft mud and slimy rocks. At other times, despite all our efforts, he tried our patience by slipping out of my arms and into the ankle-deep water. Getting him up the rocks and through the narrow cleft was difficult, and frustrating, but we achieved it.

We returned for the last time to retrieve Lady Phoebe. I knew I would have no difficulty carrying her, because she was so slight. When I lifted her, one of her arms became arched around my neck and an affected smile seemed to grace that still doll-like face. I almost let her drop. I kept glancing at her face, half expecting words to escape her lips. *You're such a beauty. You should have had a charmed life, but you picked the wrong man.*

We arrived back at the cemetery. With the aid of the torches, I laid Phoebe beside her husband's body. The combined torchlight was swung further away. They pierced the fog, to reveal uneven rows of tombstones in the background.

'Our horrific trial is over,' I thought, but Alyce lowered her torch to illuminate the four graves immediately in front of us. Four dug out graves – the end one adjoining a sealed one – had manifested. They were open and empty like grotesque lips eagerly wanting to suck us into their dark vortex. It was clear from the eroded sides and scattered weeds growing around the openings, they had been dug long ago. *We've got three bodies. Whose grave is the fourth?*

The parson put an end to those dismal thoughts. He began to explain. "When four bodies were not found after the explosion, the extra coffins were stored in that shed." The parson pointed into the night. "It's over there."

I could not fully grasp the significance of what he said, but Alyce responded by shining light over a building not far away. I thought I recognised its shape. It was the hotel garage on the block across from the hotel, or was it? I could not see any other buildings. Everything was in semi-darkness and visibility was limited. This made recognition of anything beyond our torch range impossible. Questions arose. *Why aren't there any lights on anywhere? Why isn't there anyone about? What am I thinking? It's after midnight in a small town.* But the question I most wanted answered was how Alyce seemed to know so much. This was not the time to ask.

Alyce and I hurried over to stand before the shed's large doors. I twisted the handle. It was locked. I peered closer. The lock was badly rusted. *I didn't see this shed yesterday when Mike and I got our petrol. Yesterday? It seems a lifetime ago.* I pushed against the doors. They wobbled but did not open. I picked up a rock and bashed the lock. It fell to the ground. Together we pulled the door open.

Inside the shed, the torchlight revealed four empty caskets lying side-by-side. *Coffins?* Somehow my brain refused to accept the reality of the situation. *Why would anyone keep coffins in a shed like this?* But, they seemed to be part of this macabre scene in which I was trapped.

Alyce touched me from behind. I jumped. "Greg, we need these coffins for the bodies."

"All these ... err ... *coffins?* There's only three bodies."

"Grandfather said to bring them all."

I dragged, and Alyce pushed, until they were in a line before the parson. His voice brought me back to reality. He said, "Take the lids off and place the empty coffins in the dug-out graves first, otherwise they'll be too awkward for you and Alyce to handle. The small grave's Joseph's." Obediently we pushed the four empty boxes, one by one, into the empty graves.

"The graves are ready for the bodies Greg."

I shook off the feeling of confusion and lifted Joseph. His head rested in the crock of my arm. The body seemed warm and his expression peaceful. I wanted to tell him to wake up. When I laid his body in his coffin, I placed his arms in a cross over his heart. Looking back at his face I noticed marks on his neck. I stared. It was a birthmark, called the 'mark of the victim'. *It's like mine.*

We followed the same procedure with the Westleys. Lord Westley's face was as expressionless as a white mask made out of plaster, and smooth, with no lines. It was unreal. His open eyes though still seemed alive. They stared into mine as I placed him in the coffin the parson indicated.

A loud rumbling sounded from the sky above us. Looking up I could see no clouds. Streaks of lighting accompanied the sound and seemed to spike the ground around Westley. I wondered if Westley in spirit form was out there somewhere, enjoying the spectacle.

I lowered the limp body of Phoebe into her coffin. In my haste, a brooch she was wearing hooked on to my shirt. It ripped away from her frock. I ignored it. I could not stop myself staring at her. She was still a vision of loveliness nestled in that billowing regal gown. Her beautiful porcelain face seemed to still wear a smile as if she knew some secret. Was she expecting to return? The brooch went unnoticed when Alyce spoke. "Greg hurry and cover them with earth. Time is running out."

I was called back to reality. I struggled with the lids of the three coffins and clamped them down. Two shovels appeared in Alyce's hands. She was prepared for everything. Together we threw, pushed, and scraped dirt over them, while the parson's voice droned on with prayers and blessings for the dead. His face was lowered as he read from a dog-eared prayer book. *How can he see in this light? Perhaps he knows it all by heart.* The rumbling and lightning strikes ceased at the end of the prayers.

It was when I had finished smoothing the earth over Phoebe's closed grave that I remembered her brooch. It was too late to place it in the grave with her. Not knowing what to do with it, I unhooked it and dropped it into one of my pockets.

In the light of the torch Alyce held, I stared at the respective headstones, already in place. I could barely decipher the inscriptions but I could see 'Lady Phoebe Westley' inscribed on one, and 'Lord Westley' on the next. On the third as far as I could make out, was 'Joseph Allen'. I could not brace myself to look at the name on the fourth tombstone, guarding myself against a beckoning black depression that mocked me.

"Look!" Alyce touched me lightly. She pointed into the distance, past the immediate tombstones.

Although the fog had almost completely lifted, my gaze tried hard to pierce the obscure darkness over the graveyard. Within seconds a weak moon dipping into the horizon showed up a group of figures standing amongst the tombstones. In the forefront was Harry, the barman. Other faces were also familiar. There was Jack, Bill who winked, Aunt Mavis who smiled, and Pete. They stood in a group, with the others from the town. *Why didn't they come earlier to help? At least they've had the decency to be here to witness the burial of the lost boy, and make certain the hated Westleys were well and truly despatched from this earth.*

Aunt Mavis separated herself from the group. She walked over to Joseph's grave and stood there looking lovingly down at him, and smiled. She then returned to where she had been previously.

A strange woman rose from the sealed grave next to the still empty one and floated towards Alyce and the parson. Alyce thrust the torch into my hand. "Grandma Ursula!" cried Alyce. Before the parson could move forward, Alyce and her Grandmother were in a tight embrace. *What? Where'd she come from? Hasn't she been dead for ages?*

With joy written all over his face, the parson dropped his book. He joined them. As the light lit up his face and body he seemed to be nothing but bones. He had become as a walking skin-covered skeleton. He cried with joy in his voice. "Ursula, at last." Alyce stepped back a few steps to allow them body closeness. "Dear, dear Ursula." He kissed her and she clung to him. .

I heard her whisper. "I've been waiting for you, Andy dear. I knew you would never leave me for too long."

The parson's face was awash with tears. "I should never had left. I'm sorry. I wanted to return to Rockville that night, hoping and praying you were still alive. How I tried. I tried so hard, but they wouldn't let me in."

"The waiting's over. We'll never be apart again."

The parson turned to Alyce. "I know this will be hard, but I must ask you to carry out a fourth funeral service.

"For whom?" She was puzzled but frightened as if sensing, or already knowing, the answer.

"For me."

"No Grandfather, don't ask me. Don't ask me. Don't go," Alyce pleaded as her voice started to break.

"If you don't, I could be trapped in this dimension for who knows how long. Alyce, you have to help me pass over. I should have gone ages ago, but I waited for this night for Joseph's sake, and for the people of Rockville. Please Alyce, announce the prayers and the blessing over me. My purpose has finally been fulfilled. I'm ready to join your grandmother. My grave is already waiting for me. Please Alyce."

Alyce swallowed, stood erect, proud and controlled, then slowly bent and retrieved the prayer book from the ground.

The parson stretched out his hand to grasp his wife's as he scrambled down into the remaining coffin, to stand firm and erect, while his wife remained on the top of her adjoining grave.

Alyce, her whole body shaking, took on the role of officiating at a funeral. Her experience as a lay-preacher would serve her well now. I shone the torchlight on the pages of the prayer book. She began to read. My heart ached at the stammer in her voice. After she read a few lines she stopped mid-sentence and closed the book. "I can't go on."

"Yes you can, Alyce," spoke up the encouraging voice of her Grandfather. "God bless you and Greg. God found him for us, for you . . . read on." But Alyce ran forward and clutched on to her grandparents – reluctant to let them go. The parson spoke softly into her ear. I could not hear the words. We watched as he lay down in the coffin.

Alyce returned and slowly reopened the book. Her voice was squeaky and her breath laboured. "God who is all merciful, take unto you the soul of Andrew Anderson your devoted servant. Although I go into the Valley of Death I shall fear no evil . . ."

I freaked out. "Alyce stop! Your Grandfather's not dead."

Alyce looked at me sadly, her face drenched in tears. She kept on reading. At the end of the verse, she closed the book, made the blessing over the pair as they gazed into each other's eyes. The town folk looked on.

"Ahaaa." The sound hissed out of Alyce's lips, as I stood transfixed. Before me, the bent aged body of her Grandfather appeared to take on a youthful shape and became erect. The ravaging caused over years fell from him.

"It's too late Greg. He's left us already. He's gone to join grandmother. He belongs to another era. In heaven they will always be young together."

I don't understand any of this.

Alyce allowed the prayer book to fall from her fingers, to settle still open, on the ground. She began to cry almost uncontrollably now. She leaned against me and I held her tight. No words were uttered. The new silence was only broken by her sobs as we watched the town people bow their heads. They then stepped back in unison and mounted their grave mounds. Their bodies dissolved into smoke, which was sucked down into the earth below where they were standing.

Swirling wind continued to mount dust around the parson's coffin. I panicked. I pushed Alyce aside. I was ready to leap across to the parson, to drag him out if necessary, but I was too late. He was gone, covered by the lid, which had already moved swiftly into the closed position, and its locks, without human hand, clamped down with a clanking sound. A whirly-wind spray from nowhere sucked up dirt and leaves and twigs. It eddied above the parson's grave and dropped over it.

"Grandfather died a long time ago Greg. Here, take this." Alyce handed me a shovel. Trancelike I scattered and levelled the dirt over the grave. I could do no more. I returned to Alyce's side. We stood alone now, arms entwined, heads bowed.

The sound of movement behind us made us jump simultaneously. We turned. Alyce's sobs were sniffles now. Four people, barely visible through the spreading fog eddying around them, were marching towards us. The leader wore a Military uniform. *Where did they come from?* The leader's voice became loud. It echoed in the hills around us.

"I'm Tom Allen, the last marked victim. This is John, James, and Patrick, all Allens. We were the marked victims in previous leap years. Thanks to you, Greg, and you Alyce, Westley and his wife are back in hell. He can't keep Rockville, its people, and us, between two worlds any longer. We can now start our journey to eternity." As I listened the thought came to me that Westley might somehow bribe the Devil, and return. *Don't even think it.* Tom continued, "But before we leave there is someone here Greg I'm sure you'll like to see once more . . . your Patrick." A figure came to stand beside Tom.

I gasped. "Grandfather! "

"Yes Greg. It's nice to see you again. Your grandmother is now with me and we're happy together."

"Times up," interrupted Tom. "Thank you from us, and I speak on behalf of those Allens who would have come to the same fate in future leap years." A chorus of voices reinforced his expression of appreciation. It took me moments to register what was happening. As I began to doubt the reality of what was taking place, Tom stepped back and saluted. Grandfather Patrick waved. The others were smiling as a mist rose to envelop them.

Before I could accept that my grandfather had actually appeared before me Alyce collapsed. Her limp body fell heavily against me.

I thrust out my arms to grab her and hold her upright, but I did it awkwardly and over-balanced. With Alyce still held in my arms we both crumbled. The ground seemed to spring up to meet us with force. Crashing to the road, a sharp pain spread through the same spot on my scalp as was previously hurt. Darkness, denser than the blackest night descended, blotting out all pain.

BOOK 5

THE AFTERMATH

EVIL CAN BE OVERCOME

BUT ALWAYS A PRICE IS PAID

CHAPTER 17

Excerpt from the Journal of Greg Allen.

'Greg Allen, you're a lucky man,' I said to myself as I recalled how Mike and I were able to leave Rockville and return home.
    At first, Superintendent Martino ordered that I could not leave Rockville until Mike had regained his memory of events. He wanted to arrest me on suspicion of attacking Mike. Steve Barnes, the now police academy lecturer from Straden intervened. He was the previous Superintendent at Greystone before his transfer, and when Martino was his deputy. He took away with him the determination never to retire until those responsible for the deaths in that beachfront town were before the courts. As there was no evidence to incriminate me, Superintendent Martino was forced to allow us both to leave and return to College.
    Before we left, Barnes had me promise to send him a copy of my diary when I had finished recording all we had experienced at Rockville. He believed that the answer to why Rockville was chosen by the perpetrators would lie in what I had discovered and endured there. I kept my promise. With a copy of my diary I enclosed duplicates of the photos I had taken, even though the night ones were not at all clear. After he received them he sent me his report on their discovery of Alyce and I, unconscious, on that night at the cemetery, and what led up to it. A very happy Steve Barnes has now retired.

    Today, is the 29th March 2010, two years since the horror.

Mike has not regained any memory of that visit to Rockville, which is a blessing perhaps.

Today, I am on my way to visit my wife, Alyce, who has given birth to our baby son unexpectedly early. I was still at work. I am looking forward so much to seeing baby Lyle.

At the hospital Alyce's face was full of happiness as I kissed her while handing her the flowers I had bought on the way. She sucked in her breath in delight at the roses. "I'll get a vase for them later," she said.

I looked into the crib for baby Lyle. It was empty. Alyce read my thoughts. "The nurse is bathing him. She'll bring him back soon."

I believed the Rockville ordeal was buried well beneath recent happy events, and I wanted to keep it there. It was not so deep however that it could not rise to the surface should there be any likelihood of someone in the Allen family bearing 'The Mark of the Victim'. I realised I would never rid myself of every trace of that fear the moment I was unable to prevent myself asking, "Any signs?"

She smiled happily as she replied. "No birthmarks, marks or spots even, of any kind."

The door opened and a young nurse walked in. She was carrying Lyle. As I watched her gently lay the baby into Alyce's arms, one of her short sleeves rode up her arm, to reveal more of her bare arms.

I sucked in my breath. On her right arm was a star shaped birthmark, the 'Mark of the Victim'.

"What is your name?" I asked, dreading the answer.

"Denise, Denise, Allen.

EPILOGUE

EPILOGUE
Ex Superintendent of police and retired Lecturer, Steve Barnes' Report

I COULD not erase from mind and memory, my time as Superintendent of Police at Greystone. I was stationed there during times when members of the Allen family were found dead at Rockville. The deaths began in 1992 and always occurred on the last day in February, and always in a leap year. I became determined to solve the mystery. That resolve remained, even after I had left to become a lecturer at the Police Academy in Straden. The new Superintendent, Mario Martino, who knew of my obsession, promised to call me immediately should another body be found in the leap year following my departure. I was convinced there would be.

When February 29th 2008 dawned, I was on tenterhooks, wondering if I would receive a call from Mario to say there had been another body found. As the time crawled by, my impatience grew to the extent that I could not wait any longer. Although very early for a working day I telephoned Mario, but he was not available. I left messages but when time dragged by and I had not heard from him, I gathered what items I might need and drove from Straden to Martino's Greystone office. I arrived after opening time, but the staff did not know his exact whereabouts, so I made myself comfortable in his office.

I did not have long to wait. When he saw me sitting there he grinned. He said he thought I might come, but I had wasted my time. He assured me all was quiet and he expected it to remain that way. I hoped he was right.

Late in the day, at Mario's home where he had invited me to stay, he received a call from Matron Grimshaw of the Greystone Hospital. I listened in on the call.

"Matron Grimshaw speaking, Mario."

"Why the late call?"

"A badly wounded man has been found in reception. He's unconscious and bleeding. Whoever dropped him off didn't stay or leave a note. I know it's late, but the doctor has declared it to be an attempted homicide, and to inform the police."

"Homicide? What's his name? Is he a local?"

"No, he's a uni student from Queensburg University. He's Mike Mitchell according to his driver's license, and student card."

A Mitchell, not an Allen? But it's my guess there's an Allen involved somehow.

Mario replied. "I'm on my way. Don't let any nosey reporter near him if one should arrive. I'll handle them tomorrow."

"I know my job . . . goodnight!"

Martino hastily dialled his deputy's number. "Grice, I want you to meet us at the hospital immediately. There's a suspected homicide. Matron Grimshaw has just rung me. We have to investigate this. I know it's late but bring Sergeant Norris and Senior Constable Briggs. Drag them get out of bed if you have to. Briggs can drive. Mr Barnes, your old Senior Superintendent will be with me."

"We won't be long. They're all here. We're still enjoying the barbeque we put on for my sister's birthday."

Within minutes we were on the road. Briggs made full use of the squad car siren as he drove. Once inside the hospital grounds he turned it off, and decelerated to the obligatory ten kilometres. Another car pulled out of the grounds as we were driving in.

Norris and Briggs stayed in the car as commanded by their Chief while we entered. Matron Grimshaw was annoyed at having to wait back. It was past the end of her shift so her greeting was brisk. She said, while escorting us down the corridor to the operating theatre, "Make it a very quick visit . . . Dr Young's orders." Her tone was sharp.

When we walked in, we saw the doctor and one of the nurses were in the final process of treating Mike's injuries. Dr Young turned within a few seconds. Recognizing the Chief Superintendent he nodded. "Make sure you don't touch anything," he advised us, as we joined him at the patient's side. He lifted some of the dressings for us to view Mike's injuries. Like the previous victims the unconscious man had one eye almost gouged out, a cut and a lump on his head, slash marks on his lower body, and bruises and scratches to his face. Except for the head injury and some extra bruises and scratches, he was in almost exactly the same state, as the bodies found in Rockville in previous years.

"Will he live?" I asked.

"He's lost a lot of blood and his head wounds are serious, but he's young and strong so he'll pull through. Now, if you please, I'd like you to leave."

We returned to the reception area, where Matron handed Mario a folder. She was frowning. "I'm worried about Nurse Anderson. She reported for duty on time but has not signed off. She's disappeared. She must have taken her car though. It's not in the car park. We've tried to get her on the phone but she doesn't answer. Another thing, a stranger was hanging around here yesterday. He asked about Nurse Anderson's Grandfather, but was refused information. He didn't appear to have a car. At least I didn't notice any out front."

"Could Nurse Anderson have seen who brought Mike Mitchell in and been abducted?"

"It's possible, if she was out here at the time."

Superintendent Martino turned to me. "Steve, you're wrong this time. He's not the dead Allen you expected. This is my version of what happened. Nurse Anderson saw the person who brought the injured man in. Perhaps she recognized him. To stop her giving out information, he took her hostage. He then used the nurse's own car for his get-away. What puzzles me is where the kidnapper would have left his means of transport. There's nothing parked in the car park out here. If it's a copycat attack of those previous leap year tragedies, it's the first time a victim has been brought to the hospital. That's strange behaviour for would-be murderers. Perhaps an accomplice had a late stirring of conscience, when they found it was not an Allen they had attacked. Anything's possible in this game.' I nodded in agreement as Martino turned away.

"Grice, call in Sergeant Norris."

Grice quickly obeyed. The sergeant entered briskly to receive his orders. "You are to stay behind and guard Mike Mitchell. Matron will show you which ward he's in." He turned back to the Matron. "Give me a quick description of the stranger, and Nurse Anderson's car registration number if you have it." The matron obliged by handing him a piece of paper with Nurse Anderson's car make and number already written on it. I glanced over Mario's shoulder to read it, as did Deputy Grice.

When Deputy Grice noted the details he sounded excited. He said, "That fits the yellow car that passed us on our way in. The headlights were out too".

"Then let's go. They haven't got too much of a head start." Martino was now convinced we would quickly trace, and retrieve, Nurse Anderson's car. He believed it would contain, if not Mike Mitchell's attacker, then someone known to him

Briggs had the car's engine purring over by the time the last door was shut. Martino, deep in thought, sat in the front with him. I climbed into the back seat.

I sat there silently recalling the sequence of events, four years before, when I was in charge and Martino was my deputy. A Thomas Allen, with similar wounds, including that strange shaped star cut into his stomach region, had been found dead at Rockville. Martino had moved to Greystone a month after another Allen, a Patrick Allen, was found. That case also was never solved, at least, not to my satisfaction. When I left shortly after Tomas Allen's murder, Mario had taken over.

A voice brought me back to present. "Which way Sir?" the driver asked. It made Martino hesitate.

"It's not likely they'd stay around for long. They've already dumped Mitchell at the hospital and didn't wait to see if he was okay. My guess is that they're heading towards Little Rock. They did turn the car in that direction after they passed us. That's the quickest way to get to the main highway and the big towns, where they could hide out." Martino said. He was confident they would cut the nurse's car off well before then. The little car could not compete with the speed of the patrol car, especially as the police knew every short cut to the highway itself.

A short time later, ignoring the longer route through the centre of Greystone, we cut through the local roads, and were careering along the main road towards our objective.

"Look! There's the yellow car way up ahead," spoke up Briggs as we sped on.

All of us had been constantly scanning ahead, and encompassing the fields on either side. In our search for the yellow car we could not see anything one could associate with this case.

"Won't be long now," Briggs said. Excitement rose as the distance between the two cars shortened. Martino counted aloud the heads visible through the yellow car's back window. We wondered why we could see only one head in the front while two were in the back. "He probably has an accomplice holding Nurse Anderson prisoner in the back. This time we'll get him," stated Briggs.

Martino also felt confident of success. He was convinced they were on the track of whoever left the unconscious man at the hospital. He stated again, that, if this man were not the 'Allen' murderer or would-be murderer of Mitchell, he would surely lead us to him.

The vehicle swayed from side to side as the car's route curved abruptly to avoid it crashing into the back of another car driving slowly behind a large semi-trailer.

"Watch it Constable."

Briggs acted promptly, switching on the siren. The car in front swerved to the other side of the street and disappeared from vision. "Now pass the semi. Don't lag behind!" Martino ordered. The siren continued to wail as Briggs reacted instantly, angling the car around the semi. Briggs swore as, with the narrowest of margins, he swerved quickly back behind the semi-trailer to avoid crashing into another car as it rushed towards us.

The semi-driver began to slow down. "He knows we're behind him. Why don't you pass him Briggs?"

The police car again swerved to the other side of the road to get around the semi-trailer. We all held on intently.

"Look out Briggs. Here's another speed maniac," exclaimed Martino as the still speeding car barely missed another oncoming vehicle, which zigzagged off the road. It ended in a side-sliding halt beside a farmer's fence. Martino, looking back at the car now at a standstill in the stubble on the side of the road said, "I expect there'll be a complaint lodged tomorrow at the station, although there's been no obvious damage to the car." Martino turned to look frontward again and exclaimed. "Where's that yellow car? It couldn't have taken off into space."

His companions volunteered several possibilities. The constable made the suggestion. "Wouldn't they be getting close to Little Rock by now?"

"Put more speed into it then."

The suspect car was still out of sight when Briggs pulled into Little Rock's outskirts' 'twenty-four hour' petrol station. The Sergeant leaned out of the window to ask the attendant as the car drew to a halt beside him, "Did a yellow car pass here a few minutes ago?"

The man raised his cap and scratched his mop of hair before he spoke. "I've been out here greasin' up old 'Daisy'. That's it over there." He pointed to an old truck parked against the far wall. "Nothing but a few Utes has passed by. Though there was a car, now I remember. It didn't stop. It could have been yellow, or gold. I didn't take too much notice. I was too busy with old 'Daisy.' There's a semi comin' 'long now I see. He's likely as not to come in for a bite to eat. Can I get you blokes something . . . petrol . . . food?"

"No thanks," replied Grice.

Briggs reversed sharply and accelerated quickly. The car's sudden burst of speed flung us back in our seats, and left the petrol station manager in the middle of a newly begun sentence. Briggs reduced speed as we drove through the quiet centre of the tiny town, and on into its outskirts.

Some distance had been covered when we saw what looked from the distance to be a yellow car. Martino declared, "That's it. Catch up Briggs."

When our car lights were close enough to be reflected off the back of the car ahead, Martino exclaimed, "That's gold, not yellow." Disappointment showed in his tone of voice and was echoed silently by the rest of us. "It's not the nurse's car's number plate either."

Briggs drew parallel to the gold car, keeping the same speed. All eyes stared at the driver who stared back, looking puzzled.

"There's only the driver and she's twice Nurse Anderson's size and age. No one else is in the car."

Before Martino could swear, his second-in-command remarked. "If that semi-trailer hadn't slowed up back there near the Rockville turnoff, we'd still have had the yellow car in our sights."

"Rockville, that's it!" exclaimed Martino. "That's where we found the other body. Steve, you remember, don't you?" Before I could reply, his attention had returned to Briggs! "What are you waiting for? Keep it moving." The fear of failure caused Martino's impatience to border on anger. I was disappointment, although there was still no evidence of an Allen being involved.

Briggs braked, then turned the car around to head back to Rockville. With the siren's wail invading the peace of the countryside, his foot remained weighted down. Both Martino and I shouted together, "Stop. You've passed the turn-off."

"Where?"

"Turn around! Keep awake."

The car burnt rubber as the driver swung into a U-turn, eager to correct his mistake. Meanwhile the Superintendent cursed himself for not thinking of Rockville earlier, as did I. We had been too busy attempting to intercept Nurse Anderson's car. If she had been kidnapped, there would be no better place to hole up.

"Keep your eyes peeled. I'll tell you when to turn." The Superintendent stamped his heels on the floor in agitation. "Slow down now Briggs. See that tree up there ahead? Turn left there and keep the spotlight on."

"Yes Sir, I know where I am now."

A sudden swing of the car caused its mudguard to graze some bark from the tree before it straightened up, to travel down Rockville Road. We clung on grimly to avoid our heads hitting the car's ceiling as it swayed and danced over the rut-impregnated road.

"Which way now Sir?" asked Briggs as they reached a fork in the road.

Martino was not certain. He had travelled to Rockville some time ago, but never on such a dark night. "Try left."

I spoke up, "No, right." But the car was already past the intersection.

The car bounced its way over stones and hardened mud heaps while the dark menacing face of Rockville Mountain glared down at us. The atmosphere was chilling.

"Careful Briggs, don't damage the car on any goddamn rocks or get us stuck in some ditch. We won't catch any kidnappers if we're stranded in one of these paddocks out here." Mario fell silent for a few moments before he again commanded, "Stop!"

The car jolted to a halt before a barren cliff, eroded by weather and mining machines. "We're at the quarries, not the town. Go back. Take the other branch. You should have listened to Mr Barnes."

Briggs turned the car around slowly. The Superintendent was irritated by its slow progress. I felt impatient myself, but we both knew that Briggs was a most efficient driver.

We arrived back at the fork. "How did you miss that sign lying there on the ground?" demanded Martino. "It may be ancient but it's still readable." Unable to retaliate verbally, Briggs raised his eyes to look at the roof for a second, before steering the car towards the town area.

"Look!" Their lights were now reflecting on the windows of a yellow car near an overgrown park.

"Stop on the opposite side of the road. A sniper may be hiding behind that car, so follow procedure." I was secretly pleased I had trained Mario so well.

Briggs drew the car to a standstill. He ensured that the headlights and its attached searchlight shone directly into the car. We saw no one. With guns drawn the others slunk out of the police car, crouching low. Their Chief hand-signalled his two men to move forward while I crept along beside him. After another signal Briggs trotted around the rear of the yellow car. Grice followed. We still heard and saw nothing. Briggs opened the passenger door carefully, his gun ready. "It's empty. There's no one in here," he shouted.

Grice proceeded to examine the car's interior. "There's what looks like blood stains on the driver's seat, and some at the back. I can't see any weapons, and the keys are still in the ignition." He handed them to his Chief.

Suddenly, I went cold all over as memories came rushing back. The keys of the last victim's car were still in the ignition when he disappeared. He was later found dead at the bottom of the cliff. I feared for Nurse Anderson's safety.

"Quick men. We have to check along the base of the mountain," I spoke without thinking, but Mario nodded in agreement.

We piled back in the vehicle. Its wheels crunched gravel as they barely turned, while its occupants sought any sign of movement. Our eyes glided in every direction like swallows before the rain. We saw nothing. The car rolled on until its headlights, reflecting in burnished surfaces, were flung back from the chrome plates of two discarded motorbikes. They lay on the ground near the ruins of the hotel destroyed in 1988. The car continued to crawl on for a short time, and then turned.

"On alert men . . . guns ready." The driver braked and lowered his head. The other two slid down in their seats, so as not to be sitting ducks to whoever might be out there. Nothing occurred so confidence returned. "Briggs, you get out and cover us. Keep your guns up and your heads down. If there is any serious sign of an intended attack, defend yourselves. This cowardly swine deserves no mercy. You keep with me Steve."

"Chief, over there, near the graves. There's two bodies, I think."

"Looks like the assailant's got two more. Take care. He's probably still here, perhaps watching us."

Briggs doubled up as he backed out of the car. Martino cautiously alighted. His deputy followed, then myself. Cramped in one position we waited. Five minutes on, Briggs watched as the Superintendent and his deputy crept towards the bikes. We covered their backs.

Martino, after examining the bikes, shook his head and shrugged his shoulders. Obviously he could see no damage to either, discounting a smash. He called back to us. "Perhaps they broke down, or were out of petrol, though hardly likely both would have had the same problem at the same time."

Martino remained crouched down, shielded somewhat by the bikes. He looked towards the taunting tombstones a little further away. "Come on out," he shouted in that direction. "We've got you surrounded." We waited – our nerves tight as a drum. The silence itself felt threatening. There was no response. Martino, feeling more confident, straightened up. He quickly walked with his gun in his hand towards the figures on the ground. Grice followed while Briggs remained on guard, ready for any sign of movement in the cemetery or on the road. I stayed where I was and watched. I could not interfere.

Grice produced a torch to check the faces of the unconscious pair. I remember him saying, 'It's Alyce the nurse. I recognise her. I don't know the man." Grice was feeling for a pulse. "They're both still alive. I can't see any injuries on Nurse Anderson, but the guy has blood on him. I can't see any weapon anywhere, only a . . . "

"What have you found? What's that you've got there, Grice?"

"I believe it's a prayer book Sir. It was beside the girl. There's also a cross."

Even with all my experience I was as surprised as Mario. I continued to listen. Being no longer part of this precinct I had to refrain from voicing anything I might think or feel.

"Well I've seen everything now," I remember Mario saying. "Prayers or no prayers these two have come off better than that Mitchell guy. Put the book and the cross in the car and ring for the ambulance. Then contact base and get all available men down here with searchlight gear to scout the area. The attacker may still be out there. He's probably the third person we saw in the car. For all we know there may have been a fight between the men themselves. If the attacker had then spotted us, and with the girl in a dead faint and his mate out cold, he probably panicked and ran."

Grice tossed the two items into the police car and operated the radio. He returned to his now edgy Chief. "The backup and the paramedics will be here shortly."

"Briggs, make these two as comfortable as you can with that first aid knowledge of yours. Keep alert and keep your eyes sharp. Grice and I will go back to the nurse's car. If our missing abductor is still around, he may get ideas about leaving in it. Make sure you keep alert. We don't want any more disasters. Grice will drive Mr Barnes and me to the hospital. We'll check out these two, and Mitchell if he's still alive. The sooner we arrest someone the quicker we can close the case."

I kept pace with Martino as we reached the cemetery edge. We both stared in surprise. "I'm sure there were four empty graves here," said Mario. "Now they're covered up. I haven't heard of any local deaths lately, certainly not four. I'll have to check on that when I get back to the station." I was also puzzled.

"How do I cover Briggs until the others arrive?" queried Grice standing nearby. "All those tombstones showing up like a row of huge white teeth in the half-light give me the jitters."

"Set the car lights to shine directly on Briggs. You cover him from the shadow of the patrol car until the others arrive. I'll see you later."

The first thing we did was call in at the station to quickly check certain previous reports connected to the Rockville mystery. Mitchell's injuries were very similar to the other previous victims. Checking on those now sealed graves could wait.

When we eventually arrived at the hospital we asked the Matron to give us an update on all three patients. This included the two we found unconscious shortly before. As the doctor was not accessible she had obtained the doctor's permission to pass on his latest report.

"Mike Mitchell is still recovering from an operation. Nurse Anderson is sleeping under medication, and the other man, a Greg Allen, the one who was brought in with Nurse Anderson, is still unconscious. It may be twenty-four hours before the doctor will allow an interview with any of them."

An Allen and still alive? We're back on track. I was now more optimistic about finding out the truth. He would not be going anywhere for a while. He would be encouraged to reveal everything he knew of the Rockville deaths. *It appears Martino's suspicion is correct. It must be a family feud passed down through generations.*

I will stay here indefinitely if I have to, to find out the truth about what happened that caused them to be in the condition they're in. After all the years gone by since the Leap Year deaths began, we may, after all this time, be able to bring the leap year killings to a stop.

Superintendent Martino was confident that he would have the culprit arrested and behind bars within the next few hours. "I'm certain the would-be murderer is Greg Allen, but he appears to have ended up getting the worse end of the stick," he stated.

I had grave doubts about this, as I could not dismiss the conviction that there was more to it. I believed that these Allen murders had a sinister side. I now know, after reading your diary, that I was right. It was not a fight between flawed demons. It was a struggle between demons and angels.

I now know, at long last, and with your help, no more members of the Allen family with the mark will die in Rockville. The mystery of Rockville has now been solved.

. . . .

P.S. I enclose the cross that belonged to Alyce's Grandfather, together with a prayer book with his name on it. We found it on the ground near his grave.

I also hope Alyce is happy with Lady Phoebe's brooch which I'm also sending on to you. One of the nurses found it in your pocket. I recognised it as Lady Phoebe's from a painting I am familiar with. It hangs in the Greystone Art Gallery.

BRIEF BIOGRAPHY

The prize-winning author, VERA (VERONICA) MARY MURRAY, is an ex-Pine Rivers Shire Councillor. She was born in Allora, Queensland, Australia. She has been writing since school days when she often read her poems on a radio station's Children's Hour. Her first story was published at the age of 16. When overseas she established a magazine in a vast housing estate in India. Vera formed and ran the Petrie Writers' Circle for fourteen years, creating and editing three anthologies for the group. She has held classes on creative writing for the Pine Rivers U3A (University of the Third Age) and for several other groups.

'MOVE OVER JAMES BOND and OTHER STORIES,' was published in 2010.

This book 'LEAP YEAR BLOOD LUST' is her first novel.

Printed by Libri Plureos GmbH in Hamburg, Germany